Degrees

Book 1: Saving The Earth

By

Devon G. Crowe and Timothy J. Imholt

Degrees Book 1: Saving The Earth
Echoship Gaia Press
Copyright © 2015 by Devon G. Crowe and Timothy J. Imholt
Peabody Massachusetts
For information on this and any book by the authors
contact Tim@TimothyImholt.com

ISBN-13: 978-0692408926
ISBN-10: 0692408924

For our wives and children

Books and Parts of Books by Devon G. Crowe

Non-Fiction

1. *Optical Radiation Detectors*, Eustace L. Dereniak and Devon G. Crowe, Wiley (1984).

2. *Adaptive Optics and Speckle Imaging*, Devon G. Crowe, editor, SPIE (1994).

3. "*Detectors*," Chapter 4 in Volume 3 of the *The Infrared & Electro-Optical Systems Handbook*, Devon G. Crowe, Paul R. Norton, Thomas Limperis, and Joseph Mudar, ERIM and SPIE (1993).

4. "*Increasing the bit packing density in diffraction limited optical disk storage systems*," Devon G. Crowe

Fiction

5. *Degrees Book 1: Saving The Earth* (Timothy Imholt co-author)

Books by Timothy J. Imholt

Fiction

1. *The Forest of Assassins* (David Forsmark co-author)
2. *China Bones Book 1 – China Side* (David Forsmark co-author)
3. *China Bones Book 2 – The Bamboo Caress* (David Forsmark co-author)
4. *China Bones Book 3 – The Red Pagoda* (David Forsmark co-author)
5. *China Bones – The Complete Series* (David Forsmark co-author)
6. *A Study in Scarlet with Annotations: The First Sherlock Holmes Mystery* (annotations by Timothy Imholt)
7. *The Sign of the Four with Annotations* (annotations by Timothy Imholt)
8. *The Hound of the Baskervilles (Annotated)* (annotations by Timothy Imholt)
9. *The Valley of Fear (Annotated)* (annotations by Timothy Imholt)
10. *Degrees Book 1: Saving The Earth* (co-author Devon G. Crowe)

Non-Fiction

1. *The Layman's United States Constitution* (Michael Garst coauthor)
2. *The Layman's Articles of Confederation* (Michael Garst coauthor)
3. *Laughing at a Military Enlistment* (Michael

Garst coauthor)

4. *Fighting Spirit* (Tom Duggan coauthor)

Preface

This novel draws on the classic science fiction theme of human intervention in phenomena that were formerly the exclusive province of Nature. This theme is driven by a vision of the Earth as an integrated system that contains all of the *known* life in the universe, including humanity. Planet Earth (also known as Space Ship Earth and The Pale Blue Dot, among other monikers signifying a finite shared habitat in space) is affected by the activity of the humans who inhabit it. This novel concentrates on global warming and climate change. It is agnostic with respect to the cause of global warming, although we recommend reading a suggestive set of publications [1] that examines this issue in depth. Regardless of the cause of global temperature change, the protagonist of this novel endeavors to control it on a planetary scale. The unity of our planet, that is shared by all of humanity and all other life as we know it, is symbolized for us by the song, "We Are One," performed by Kelly Sweet [2].

Many of the events and theories contained in this narrative are highly speculative fiction that resides outside established science. However, some of these science speculations were suggested by, or extrapolated from, publications in the relevant literature. One of us (Devon Crowe) acknowledges first hearing about reducing insolation using optical devices located at a Sun-Earth Lagrange point from Roger Angel [3], inflatable UV-cured rigid space structures from Prakash Joshi [4, 5], and the slingatron accelerator from many enjoyable conversations with Derek Tidman [6-25]. For readers who may be surprised at the speculation in this book that The University of Arizona will be ranked first nationally in the National Science Foundation Rankings for Expenditures in the Physical Sciences in 2030, we note that this university was already ranked first nationally in this NSF category in 2008 [26].

We offer a special acknowledgement with our gratitude to Jessica Franken for improving the Second Edition with her valuable suggestions and proof reading. Any remaining errors in this book are of course the responsibility of the authors.

Devon G. Crowe

Timothy J. Imholt

Chapter One

- "Everyone suffers some injustice in life, and what better motivation for hard work than to help others not suffer in the same way." - Bella Thorne

Ken Hallbar was thinking about that day thirty years ago when he was nervously reporting for his first day of work at this hotel. Back then he had been a valet, spending his days parking the luxury and high performance cars that rich visitors from all over the world favored, especially when they were on holiday trips. That had been a fantastic holiday season. It was 1999 and in a few weeks the world would celebrate a new century, while nervously waiting to see if every computer in the world was going to stop working because of some possible bug he didn't completely understand.

That seemed like a long time ago now.

That was way back when he was in prep school. Back then his largest problem was trying to decide if he should go to college, or just continue to work at the hotel. His father had warned him that it would mean a lot of hard work and even then he might not go very far. He would have no formal higher education, and he was starting at the bottom.

He had argued with his father, saying that they were living in paradise. Tahiti was a very hard place for him to leave, even temporarily.

Now, that he was the general manager, he was very pleased with the path he had taken.

The guest experience, that he was instrumental in creating, along with the clear skies, warm weather, an inviting beach, and amazing waters for diving, should mean that the *Hotel Éternal* would fetch a premium this time of year for any room, much less the deluxe gazebos out over the water. A full hotel would have meant that he would have been taking calls to apologize that no more rooms were available for last minute travelers. As he gazed outside, the sun was shining, there was a slight breeze, and the temperature was a little bit lower than normal but, in general, it looked just like it should for this time of year.

That was all about to change. According to the news, the barometric pressure was falling rapidly, and that meant that a storm was coming, a very large one. Some of the locals were already saying it was going to be a "once in a generation" weather event. These were people who had nothing better to do than sit around talking about the weather.

The weather forecasts all predicted a storm of monumental proportions. According to them, this would be one of the largest weather shifts ever recorded. It was going to go from bliss to hell on Earth. He sighed to himself with the thought that he had called this breathtaking island his home for his entire life, and no mere weather front was going to get him to leave this island.

Maybe he was just getting old, but he thought that the weather was behaving strangely lately. The gradual changes as a storm came in that normally gave people time to react were no longer a guarantee. A scientist had appeared on the news to explain why, but then another one showed up and said the first one was wrong, then someone else said that all scientists agree. The observation that even these two were in disagreement seemed lost upon those claiming there was universal agreement. Ken scoffed, he had never heard of absolute agreement upon any subject.

As a hotel manager he didn't care about any of that. His only thoughts were about the guests, or the lack of guests.

There had been discussions about global temperature changes and environmental impact for so long that he, like many people, had stopped listening. Climate change they called it. There were claims that if mankind didn't change its ways, bad things would happen, maybe, perhaps, someday, but no one was sure how soon. Like most people he didn't pay attention to what might or might not happen, at a future date yet to be determined, because no one is sure when, or even if, it will occur. It seemed odd to him that the claims always seemed to be made by a scientist who was only able to successfully explain the situation to other scientists. Non-scientists would just never understand it. At least that was the way it seemed to him.

Given the situation about to unfold, he couldn't help but wonder if one of the two were right. Perhaps the storm barreling down on them to destroy the holiday season for his guests was part of whatever it was that they had been arguing about for decades. He dismissed the thought as irrelevant, because none of that really mattered, and all of it was beyond his control.

There was only one thing that mattered right now. The guests were leaving in droves. As manager, he should be able to find a way to convince them to stay, but so far all of his attempts had been 100% unsuccessful.

He did everything he could, tried every trick he had learned over the years to keep them happy. But the coming heavy rain, and strong winds that were now being forecast for Tahiti were combining to be far more persuasive than he could ever be.

Why shouldn't they leave? Most of his guests had their own airplanes and could come and go as they pleased, on a moment's notice. Many of them had even paid for their pilots to bring along their own families to stay at the hotel, meaning that each early departure was twice as painful.

He cursed cyclone Cladis. The edge of the storm was expected to pass over his home, turning the island paradise into a place where no one would want to be. By all accounts any resemblance to paradise would be gone, at least temporarily. He had lived here long enough to know that storms come and go. This one may be big, but it too, would pass.

To rub salt on the wound, it wasn't just the storm. The cleanup would take weeks, if not months. No, he thought to himself, this was it for at least a month.

He glanced across the lobby toward the bar, and

away from the coffee lounge. This time of morning the bar was closed, but he had turned on the televisions so that he, and anyone else who walked by, could monitor the weather.

With a sigh he realized that he would have to resign himself to a much smaller year-end bonus. At least he would get to spend more time with his wife, Adena Eliana Hallbar.

In hushed whispers many people said she was just a trophy wife, but to him she was much more. Those comments always made him wonder who he was to deserve such an awesome trophy. She was not just a former model, turned Oscar winning actress, who now promoted both the Island of Tahiti and the hotel. She was the love of his life, and as intelligent as she was attractive.

He considered himself an extremely lucky man.

There was an added personal bonus this year. Being able to spend time with his daughter would more than make up for the financial loss. They had enough money anyway, to hell with the bonus. His wife made far more in a year than he could ever dream of making in his career. He had no complaints. It merely brought him a sense of accomplishment to add to the family income in some fashion, however meager by comparison. It was important for his feeling of self-worth to be productive.

He was really looking forward to their daughter's visit over the school holiday. He hoped she could arrive home before the storm cancelled all the inbound flights. She had been away at prep school for what seemed like an eternity. He knew it had only been a few months, and she had gone away for semesters many times before, but he always missed her when she was gone.

He and a perennial repeat guest were the only two in the lobby. It was a gorgeous lobby with marble tile flooring, original paintings by local artists, and some amazing local flowers that produced an exotic effect. He always thought of those flowers as things that grew in his garden effortlessly, but the marketing was better if they were called exotic. There was something about the local environment that made them very hearty here, yet difficult to grow elsewhere. He supposed exotic was as good a word as any.

The guest was watching the weather forecast in the coffee bar and relaxing in an overstuffed leather armchair. He spoke loudly from across the lobby, "Hey Ken, the storm is turning, and this thing is going to hit sooner, and more directly than anyone thought. I am calling to get my plane ready. Can you check me out today?"

"No problem at all," he said barely suppressing a sigh of disappointment. "We look forward to seeing you again next year. Hopefully you will be able to stay throughout the entire holiday next time."

Just outside the hotel entrance was the valet parking desk, it was right next to a wonderfully landscaped garden space. He glanced in that direction and noticed that the trees were bending more severely in the breeze than they were just a few minutes ago. He guessed that the forecasts were probably right and the storm would hit sooner than expected.

Under the covered reception station the valet manager was doing his best to direct both vehicle traffic and his valets through the mass exodus of guests. They all seemed to be checking out at the same time.

Inside the hotel, thanks to automated checkout, he rarely had a departure line at the desk, but this morning he had taken desk duty to free up every possible set of hands to assist the departing guests. They might be leaving, but he would do whatever could be done to ensure that process was easy for them. Normally departures naturally staggered themselves throughout the morning, but in their attempts to avoid the storm, the guests made it appear as though the hotel had just been given a mandatory evacuation order.

The weather man was saying that it was going to be a challenge to leave town before the airport closed, but people were doing their best. Maybe his daughter might not make it for the holiday after all. As long as she was safe, he didn't mind waiting a little longer to see her.

The *Hotel Éternal* was the most recently renovated on the island. The renovation had created an eleven-story main building, which was an exceptional achievement in Tahiti. Locals referred to it as the high rise. Many of the guests came from places where this was considered short, but here it was an exception. The structure was built upon steel and composite reinforced concrete pillars. These pillars were driven deep into the bedrock. The hotel was built so strongly that it was a refuge, or a safe haven, for people to occupy when it was necessary to ride out storm surges. Serving as a storm shelter was part of the deal made with the local government to allow its construction. Normally they wouldn't allow something so large for fear of destroying the exotic look of the Island that attracted the tourists here. The majority of the local economy was based on these visitors, and nothing would be permitted that would chase them away.

He was so lost in thought that he didn't realize what was happening outside. He took no notice of the wind increasing to outright windy, bordering on dangerously so. Had someone told him what was coming next, he wouldn't have believed it. It wouldn't have mattered, it was too late to do anything about it.

Suddenly, without warning, he heard a commotion outside. He looked toward the floor to ceiling windowed entrance and saw some people frantically running away from the beach. They were dropping their belongings, picking up their children and screaming as they went as fast as they could move their feet.

In all of his years working here he had never seen anything like this. It was so out of the place that he watched it in disbelief unsure how to react.

Those outside the hotel knew what it was. Their knowledge couldn't save them. When Mother Nature threw a temper tantrum there was very little mortal man could do to stop it.

They saw the thirty-meter tall rogue wave rushing toward the hotel. It was a lethal wall of water that appeared suddenly, and without warning.

The fast moving water was bringing an enormous amount of energy along for the ride. That energy was going to go somewhere. It would only be dissipated when whatever the wave hit was destroyed, and it didn't care if that was a hotel, a Ferrari, or a human.

It was still more than fifteen meters tall and moving quickly when it reached the hotel entrance.

As the wave passed the front of the hotel all of the valet staff, guests, every single one of the expensive cars, and anything else that was freestanding, were all swept away while being smashed into pieces by the surge of water. What wouldn't float was submerged in that fast moving wall of pain.

Rooms as high up as the fifth floor were rapidly filling with water before most of the guests inside could find the door to exit the room. The few who did find those doors learned that they were impossible to open. In the struggle of human strength versus rushing water, the water was winning. They were trapped by the very ocean they had come to enjoy.

Guests on the sixth floor and above watched helplessly in a mixture of horror and disbelief as water rushed by below their window and carrying the crumbled remains of ocean villas. Among the wreckage some of the broken bodies of the guests could be seen floating along like just one more piece of broken wood.

***

In the eleventh floor penthouse above the hotel, Adena Eliana Hallbar panicked. She rushed to the phone to call her husband to warn him to get to the higher floors immediately.

There was no dial tone.

She saw for herself what was happening on the video monitor that continuously displayed the entrance to the hotel, as well as the beach in front. It had seemed like a scene from one of her early movies, back when she still made horror films.

She ran to her computer. She looked to see if her daughter was online, she wasn't.

She opened the app for recording a video message and made sure she was centered in the frame for the webcam to record a message for Emma. It would automatically go to their shared cloud account for her to be alerted once it was saved. Hopefully she would see it within minutes.

"Emma, we are being hit by some kind of huge wave. I'm not sure where your father is. It is massive. The hotel is shaking, the cabanas are gone. I saw cars being thrown inland like they were the marbles you used to shoot around our house. Do not come to the island. Stay where you are, it isn't safe here on the…"

Her words were cut off by the windows being blown in. The wind had become too much for the reinforced glass. Normally the actress could have continued to work despite the distraction, she had been in enough action movies. In this case it wasn't possible.

A large, jagged chunk of glass had lodged itself in her neck. Arterial blood spurted in pulsating red streams. It spewed around the room, painting the walls with a red mosaic. She was still centered in the frame as she collapsed to the floor, clutching her neck. The camera automatically panned keeping her in the center. She clutched at her neck, pressing hard, but no amount of pressure on this wound would have helped. As she fell her head became unbalanced, as the glass had nearly severed it from her body. Her spinal cord could be seen, and as she fell it severed completely. Her head rolled out of sight, leaving her decapitated body in full view. The final pint of blood spurted from her neck and then became a trickle. A moment later the roof collapsed and buried her under thousands of pounds of concrete and steel. The last data to reach the cloud from her video conference was the explosive sound of the roof hitting the floor as her headless, blood-drained corpse disappeared under the wreckage.

***

Up above a helicopter captured the wave, as well as the inundation of the hotel's lower floors, on video. It was a tourist helicopter that recorded its tours, and occasionally sold video to television news programs. The pilot gripped his controls tighter as he saw the building start to tilt. He tried to keep the picture centered, while fighting the urge to fly away as fast as possible. He could not believe what he was seeing. Surely it was an optical illusion caused by their motion in the air and the rapid passing of the wave carrying all that debris. There was simply no way to cause a building that size to tilt just because a wave hit it. It was just water, surely the building was stronger than water.

The pilot could no longer deny reality. The building tilted further, slowly at first, then it picked up speed as it fell into the water. He could see that sparks were flying from electrical wires, pipes started pushing through the wall, and even furniture could be seen as it was ejected from the wreckage.

Water splashed unimaginably high when the giant concrete walls split apart and fell in the water. The roof exploded outward throwing large sections in all directions. What remained of the building looked more like a massive pretzel being twisted and prepared for the oven by a baker than a building.

The trees that once lined the approach to the building were now either underwater, or being carried along with the rushing tide. Some of them had been ancient and so deeply rooted that the pilot pointed them out to the tourist passengers, they were so huge he couldn't believe it. He could not imagine how much force must have hit them to uproot them, as well as topple a building, and carry off the entire set of villas that had once been out in the bay. Much of the debris was now some hundred meters inland and moving fast.

Suddenly a raindrop hit the canopy, then another.

Out of nowhere the rain that had been a mist for just a few seconds shifted into high gear and became a torrential downpour. The wind went from the few knots it had been when he had taken off less than an hour before and was now gusting at what felt like fifty knots and increasing.

He couldn't be sure how fast the wind was, his instruments were showing all kinds of crazy things. He could not believe that the wind gusts were exceeding one hundred knots, it had to be an instrumentation problem. That just didn't happen here. Not in Tahiti, not when the air had been so calm just a few moments before.

He said as calmly as he was able, with a higher than normal pitch in his voice as he spoke into the intercom to the passengers, "We have to get out of here. We MUST get back to the airport and land! I can't keep us in the air with this kind of wind. God help those people."

An even larger gust of wind hit the side of the aircraft sending it in a new direction. He fought the controls but it was useless. The wind was far too powerful for the small helicopter. They were going down.

The pilot tried to pull up. It hit the side of the building and broke apart on impact. It was now just one more pile of rubble in the rushing water.

***

The National Weather Service Regional Office in Hawaii was tracking the storm carefully. The director spoke softly to himself, "1,800 miles across. How did you grow so damn fast?" he always talked to storms as though they were people.

"Just an hour ago you were just one third that size. Good, good it will miss us. Oh no...Tahiti..."

He reached over to his cellular phone. He had to alert people in Washington. This was going to be a disaster that needed rescue and recovery teams to be sent in to help. There would also have to be press releases. The world would want to know about this, and he was never one to want to speak to the press. He was not sure how press spokespeople managed something like this disaster. They had to say something that softened the truth.

The truth was that many people were going to die.

There was some strange data that he didn't understand coming from instrumented buoys in the ocean near Tahiti. He couldn't believe that waves that size were generated by a storm. If those data points were real, that would mean the waves hitting Tahiti were larger than any recorded at that location before.

The first priority was the storm warning. Then he could take the time to study the data and figure out where the error was coming from.

Chapter Two

Emma was looking out the taxi window watching the scenery go by. She was relieved to finally be getting some vacation time. It was a long awaited break from daily life, a chance to get away from school and relax for a while.

She had just finished her next-to-last semester as a prep school student. Life had been hectic for longer than she could remember, but as a student who was driven to be the best at whatever she did, that was to be expected. There was always another paper to write, or preparation for another test, until today, and unfortunately it would be much too short of a break.

She was looking forward to the holidays. She missed her parents, missed her friends, and going home to Tahiti was always relaxing. There was important news, and it was something she wanted to do face-to-face. She had recently been accepted into a fantastic undergraduate program in neuroscience that could lead to a graduate program and perhaps even to Medical School.

Acceptance into this University program would put her on a path that she hoped she would enjoy while helping others, as well as provide a way to make a good living. Merely being accepted into the program made her excited. She really wanted to make her own way in the world and not be dependent on her parent's financial good will.

Her academic advisor told her that she had a wide range of talents, but not all of them would enable a well-paid career. Her interests included playing piano, popular dance, and medicine. At the urging of her parents, and with a small dose of reality, she had chosen medicine.

Even in grade school she had thrown herself into her schoolwork. Her grades had been impeccable, and she had wanted to take every science and math class possible. When the time came for preparatory school, her parents had sent her to a boarding school that far exceeded the educational experience one could expect to find on Tahiti.

She spotted the airport in the distance, and became more and more excited as it got closer with each passing moment.

Since finishing her final exams, she had shut out all news broadcasts. She liked to keep up with what was going on in the world, but she often found the reporting stressful and the holidays were a time for stress relief. To her the world seemed to be such a mess recently. She supposed it didn't help that her school was located just outside of Washington DC, the center of political games for the country.

Once she landed on the island, she would feel much better. Tahiti had a way of making anyone surrounded by all of that natural beauty feel like all was right with the world, and all of their worries could wait.

She couldn't wait to tell everyone that she had chosen a career path. It had been a subject of some drama in her life as her parents were urging her to make a decision. They urged her to start working toward something, even if it later changed, just pick a direction and start.

She could hear her father now. He would say something like, "At last! We have a decision! Hallelujah!"

The cab pulled up outside the departures terminal, she paid the driver for the trip along with a generous tip, got her luggage out of the trunk, and rolled it inside. There appeared to be almost no traffic at the international departures terminal. That seemed unusual, but she took it as a blessing.

Once she got inside, she discovered that there was no line at all for the ticket agents. She thought that was a little bit odd, but it gave her a chance to talk to a human being instead of the self-service check in. Electronic ticketing replaced most of the human agents before she was old enough to travel by herself, but she preferred the personal touch when it was available. It was how her father ran his hotel, and she always felt it was the best form of customer service.

"Emma Hallbar," she said as she handed her identification card and a copy of her reservation information to the ticket agent.

"You are trying to go to Tahiti for the holidays?" inquired a puzzled ticket agent looking at her reservation.

"Yes, I am going home to spend the holidays with my family and friends," she replied.

The agent looked at her with even more disbelief, "I am afraid that all flights to that area are delayed or cancelled because of the weather. In fact, most international flights going just about anywhere are in the same status at the moment because of what is going on in that part of the world. We really don't have any kind of information on when they will resume. Please leave your contact information, since you didn't elect our automated notification system when you bought your ticket. The automated system will call you with any updates when we have them."

"I don't understand. Shouldn't I just wait here? How long can the delay because of a little weather possibly last? I hate to go all the way back to my apartment if I'm just going to have to turn around in a few hours," she said.

"Ma'am, have you not seen the news?" asked the agent in a slightly hushed tone with her head tilted slightly trying to force a smile and failing. The result of the agent's attempt at delivering what appeared to be bad news, without having to deliver the specifics, was that she ended up looking confused. Emma thought that something about this was different than anything she had dealt with before.

"No, I tuned out a few days ago, and stopped watching the news, or anything really. I haven't even looked at social media. But I talked to my parents last night and they didn't say anything was out of the ordinary," she replied becoming a little confused.

"You should really look into what is going on there. Apparently things have changed quickly, turning very bad. In just the past two or three hours things are much different than they were last night. The situation there is apparently pretty serious at the moment," said the agent. The woman appeared to want to say something else but held back.

Emma couldn't help but notice that the ticket agent was speaking in very generic terms although she appeared to know some specifics. That made her very apprehensive and a little nervous. Something about the way the woman spoke made her stomach start to fill with butterflies.

"Ok," she replied writing down her number for entry into the automated callback system before slowly walking away from the counter concerned about what to do next, or even where to go. Surely there would be flights resuming in a few hours. These storms popped up from time to time, but they always passed the island quickly. It was such a long flight with a layover, why would they stop her at the point of origin? Why stop all international flights because of a little storm in the South Pacific? She had a growing list of questions with no answers. It was time to find out what was going on.

She found a table at the closest restaurant, ordered some lunch, got out her tablet device along with the 3-D glasses and started an internet search to solve these mysteries. She was certain that she could find out what was happening, estimate how long the delay was going to be, and hopefully avoid a trip back to her apartment.

Once connected she saw that there was a video message for her from her parents account. Maybe that would explain what was going on.

At first she thought she was looking at a joke. Surely it was some hoax or comedy website thinking they were being funny.

Then she realized it wasn't a hoax. Her mother had been trying to record a message when something exploded and…she couldn't believe her eyes. Her father missing, and her mother dead, as she watched.

There was so much blood, so much chaos. How could it be real? How could it happen to her?

Emma realized this had to be real, but that didn't make it any easier to believe.

She felt like she wanted to throw up. Her stomach was doing flips. She could feel her breakfast start to come up. Tears were freely flowing down her face. She had no idea what to do. She had no idea what to do. She was alone in the world with no place to go.

She covered her face with her hands. Sobs wracked her body. The airport staff and the few other patrons looked at her…she didn't care.

Her phone rang. She still was trying to process the image of her mother being decapitated, not wanting to believe it was real.

"Hello?" she said with her voice shaking.

"Is this Emma Hallbar?" asked the male voice.

"Yes," she said.

"Emma, my name is Travis from MSNBC, please tell us what how you feel about your mother's death. The video is everywhere and the world wants to know how you are doing," he said.

"What? I just saw…How. What are you talking about?"

"The video has been on every channel for the last hour, it has more hits per hour on social media than anything else at the moment, and our viewers want to know, how do you feel knowing that your parents are both fatalities caused by climate change?"

"I have no idea what you are talking about! My mother was just killed and you want to know how I feel about climate change!" she screamed and hung up.

What she didn't know was that one of the largest cyclones ever recorded had just hit Tahiti head on.

She looked at a weather station to figure out just what the hell was happening there. Was this a hoax? Were her parents really dead? Was her mother really crushed?

Growing up on the island she was used to storms, but this one was making her break out in a cold sweat just looking at the imagery. She saw that they were reporting that this storm was surpassing all storm records, not just for Tahiti, but for the entire world. It was putting out 300 mile per hour wind gusts with ten-minute sustained winds of nearly 225 miles per hour. There were reports of tsunami-scale waves of unbelievable size. Some of them measured over 125 feet in height. Somehow it was holding together as a storm system while measuring 1,800 miles across. That just didn't make any sense, even she knew that. It looked like Mother Nature had just declared war on Tahiti, and had no intention of losing the battle.

She found the page that showed the track the storm was taking. It was headed straight for Tahiti. It looked like only about 10% of the storm had gone across the island so far. The storm was over 1,800 miles in diameter and only the first 200 or so had gone over the island. It looked like the island was located at the dead center of the storm track, meaning that the entire storm would be hitting her home. It wouldn't be a glancing blow, Tahiti was going to feel the full force of this monster storm called Cyclone Cladis.

She followed the link for damage reports to see how bad it was, she quickly scanned, hoping to find a list of survivors. Maybe her parents would be on that list and she was jumping to conclusions. They had to be alive, it just couldn't be possible that she was alone in the world so suddenly.

She found a series of composite satellite radar and photographic images showing the island with hotel names superimposed over giant piles of rubble. The radar data was not the kind of imagery the eye was used to seeing, so the National Weather Service altered pre-storm images in the computer to agree with the radar data. It appeared as though the viewer was seeing a cloud-free image of the storm damage.

There it was...The *Hotel Éternel*. What was left of it was over on its side.

That wasn't supposed to be possible the way that place was built. Surely they had the labels wrong.

She zoomed out on the map looking for landmarks.

There was the bay, the road, what was left of the high school...there was no doubt. That was her home. It was lying on its side.

Her parents...her family, dead.

Her whole body went cold. She broke out in a sweat. Her heart raced in her chest, it felt like it was going to jump out.

She felt like she was going to fall to the floor.

What was she to do?

She was sure that the call for a rescheduled flight would not come anytime soon, not that she had a home to return to.

***

Doctor Phillip Stone had been the head of the National Oceanic and Atmospheric Administration (NOAA) for a few years. He had achieved this position largely as a result of his well-known work on understanding climate change. More specifically, he was considered to be the world's foremost authority on the sources of climate change. He had been objective in his research. He had presumed mankind innocent until the evidence showed otherwise, but in the end the verdict was clear. He had published that while climate change could be due to natural processes, with a high degree of certainty it did appear to be caused, at least in some small part, by our species. There was still a chance that humankind was innocent but, in his opinion, it was a very small probability. Not that it mattered. The climate was changing and arguing over who was at fault was not going to change the fact that it was shifting, and not for the better where humans were concerned.

He had seen enough simulation and modeling results to reach one hard conclusion: it was probably already too late to alter the fate of the climate without some unaffordable and massive series of interventions.

The models were very sensitive to their underlying assumptions and initial conditions. Some were even chaotic in their predictions. But on average, the warming indications were clear. In any location on any given day, it might be either warmer or cooler than usual. Only the long-term global average warming was consistent among the various sets of predictions.

He had always suspected that there was a threshold of pollutants beyond which change would occur more rapidly. He now saw evidence that this threshold had been exceeded, or so it would seem. He had never known when it would happen, but he thought that he was looking at it.

Some said that it was a natural carbon cycle, perhaps some kind of chemical reaction caused by the solar cycle. Others said it had to be mankind. Right now all of that was irrelevant.

No cyclone of this size had ever been recorded. These storms had not formed as quickly in the past as this one had just done. They had always come with warning signs, but this one did not. It was big, it was fast, and it would kill almost anything that got in its way.

Storms were typically limited by their surrounding environment to a maximal size. Once they got past that size they would either diminish or break apart. It takes an enormous amount of energy to fuel a storm system as it gets larger. This storm had exceeded all expectations for a cyclone in the Pacific Ocean. Phil Stone was in awe. He thought they needed a new word to describe this class of storm. Cyclone did not seem adequate.

He wasn't sure how long it would take but he was sure that sooner or later his phone would ring and the President's scheduler would be on the other end of the line. From that moment on he would only have a few hours to prepare a briefing for his boss. He was starting to pull together notes on what would be in that briefing when it happened.

The one question he knew would be asked was, what can be done do to stop it? Now that the changes can no longer be denied, what program can be put in place to reverse the course and put things back the way they were?

He knew the correct answer but he couldn't think of a good way to phrase it. The only thing he could come up with was, "Nothing Mr. President. All you can do is to get out of the way when storms like this happen. When a storm this size appears, hopefully you are somewhere else."

He had no other answer than to get out of the way. He didn't like telling the President to run. That was an answer he didn't like and one he was sure his boss would hate. Both of them liked solutions. Get out of the way was not a solution.

He would deliver the bad news, and then he would resign his position. Scientists were supposed to have answers. They were supposed to know how to fix problems, and for the first time in his life he had no acceptable answer.

Chapter Three

Emma's world was destroyed. She was destroyed. She had no place to go. Her home, gone. The one place that felt somewhat comforting, her dorm room, which she always called an apartment, was closed for the holidays. Locked out of her only sanctuary, she stood outside the airport terminal and suddenly realized she was more alone than ever.

She had no idea what to do. Should she call a classmate? They had all gone home.

Her options seemed so small and she was powerless. She had never felt this way, ever.

She choked back the tears. She had to. It was a matter of survival. She tried to reach for her phone, but it was inside her bag and her hands were shaking so badly she wasn't sure she could dig around in there and find it.

Worse, she was cold. The weather had turned, but she was dressed for Tahiti, which should have been her destination. She always flew dressed for where she was going when she traveled.

Washington DC was going to have to be home for the moment.

She grabbed a cab and decided returning to the school was the only choice. She would have to find a way to get back into her room.

As the airport disappeared into the distance she felt the door closing on what had been her life. Now, she had no idea what life really meant.

Hopefully the school could be opened and she would have a place to stay. She wasn't sure, given her age that she could even check into a hotel without an adult. Hopefully she could get in. Right now the image of her mother being killed by flying glass kept going through her head. She couldn't think of anything else. Her imagination was running wild with what happened to her father, and all of the options she could come up with were worse than the last.

She finally managed to take out her phone and dialed the headmaster. She probably should have done that before taking a cab to her school, but she really had no place else to go, so this had to happen, she had to get in.

"Doctor Scott, it's Emma Hallbar, I don't know if you remember me," she said choking back tears.

"Of course I do Emma, I saw the video of your mother and I can't imagine what you are going through. Please return to the school. I will meet you at the dorm and let you in, unless you want to come to my residence. I will be making lunch in a little bit if you would like something to eat, or even if you just need someone to talk to," he said with sympathy in his voice.

"Thank you but I think I would really rather be alone for a little while," she said, not sure that she believed it.

Once back in her room, she paced the floor for a few minutes, not sure what to do next. She finally gave in and turned on her 3-D full immersion television along with her computer. Maybe there was some good news. Perhaps her father was just missing, and could be found. The video from her mom merely said that he couldn't be reached, the rest of what her mom had to say she couldn't begin to imagine. Every time she thought of her mom her hands started to shake and she needed to sit. How was it possible she was dead…from flying glass? How had her life gone from being well planned to this chaos in seconds?

When she was sitting in the airport and seeing it on the portable glasses it wasn't the same. Her home entertainment unit allowed her to walk through the scene. For television shows that was fun, but for this it was just horrific. Then it hit her.

How did the video get out? Someone had to have hacked into their Cloud account! Her mom was always followed by voyeuristic paparazzi or rabid fans, but this was a new record for invasion of privacy. She felt violated in ways that the loss of her parents didn't. She fell to the floor with tears flowing rapidly down her face soaking her shirt. How could they have done this? Who were these sick bastards? How the hell did they sleep at night?

At least they hadn't figured out where she was. She hoped they wouldn't. They would ask questions about her mother, and she was so numb that she just wanted to lie down on the floor and scream.

She momentarily thought there might be a way to find something good. Perhaps her father had survived and she just didn't know it yet. That turned out to be hopeless. Everything she saw coming from the region was dominated by replay after replay of the image of her mother.

She had been so absorbed by the hope that someone she knew was going to call that she lost all track of time. She had been back in her room for hours when she realized it was now 9 PM and she hadn't eaten since hours before her aborted attempt for lunch at the airport. The dorm kitchen was closed. She had a microwave, a refrigerator and a coffee pot in her room, but no food. There was no way she was going to go shop, so she ordered delivery food from the Chinese place. Delivery had the advantage that a drone would bring it to her window. That way she would never lose sight of her television. Maybe someone she knew was alive. Maybe her home would be spared, at least in some small way.

There were constant announcements of breaking news, but all the reports had the same content that they had been talking about for hours, just with some new way to describe the destruction.

Once in a while she would try to look away. She even thought she was going to throw up the small amount of delivery food she had managed to eat. She hadn't even bothered finishing, there was no chance that was going to happen.

The news director would break in from time-to-time to show a rescue team preparing for takeoff, but they couldn't go in to provide any help until the storm passed, or at least subsided a little. That would be at least another day or so.

After what had to be twelve hours of the same

information, the climate change scientists began to arrive.

There was some good news for getting any useful information, she thought sarcastically.

These scientists seemed to be arguing about who was at fault for what just happened. Who was at *fault*? It was a storm. How could someone be at fault?

They wanted to sit around and pontificate about who was behind the death of thousands of people? Why couldn't they shut up and get some news out about survivors, you know, something that matters!

She wasn't sure if her father was alive or dead, or if any of her friends had survived, and they want to point fingers. Right now there are problems, and those morons want to assign blame to some industrial consumption of fossil fuels generating electricity as they sit in a comfortably air conditioned studio surrounded by electric lights.

Genius argument!

She did not care right now if someone was to blame, that was irrelevant. The storm was happening. Rescuing as many people as possible was the important thing. Making sure people were safe was infinitely more important to her than assigning blame.

One of the experts claimed that mankind's extensive and long-term use of fossil fuels had changed the climate so extensively that there was no longer a valid understanding of how to predict what was going to happen. He went on to say that unless we curb the use of these fuels immediately, storm systems of this kind would become worse and more frequent. She wasn't sure he could make that claim and in the same breath claim that all of the understanding of how to make predictions was not valid. Wasn't his statement a prediction? Perhaps that was lost on this "expert."

The scientist went on at some length to explain that the situation may be so dire that even if humans changed their ways immediately, it may already be too late.

The other scientist on the panel seemed to take a different position and said that climate change was a natural process and it would happen in spite of how the human race generated energy. He claimed that all we had to do was improve our computer models, and then we would understand what happened. These improved models would allow us to predict these storms in the future. He claimed that this was just part of life on planet Earth, and we would have to expect these storms. He said this super storm was an anomaly that probably wouldn't occur again for thousands of years. It wasn't merely the storm of the century, in his mind it was the storm of the millennium. It was a storm, he said, that we would probably never see the likes of again.

She didn't care how it was labeled, this storm had killed people. It wasn't an academic exercise to be argued over, it was real life. It was her life and the end of her mother's. Then, in between the arguing about blame, they would go back to talking about her mother's death and show the stolen video footage, not mentioning that they had invaded her family's privacy to get it.

Some part of her wanted to start screaming at the people who put it on television. Then she realized it was already on the net and was now never going to be contained or shut down. Anyone who wanted to see it would be able to do so forever.

Her phone rang. She didn't recognize the number but hoped it was news of her father.

"Hello, dad?!" she said hopefully, butterflies started jumping around in her stomach. Could he really be alive?

"Is this Emma Hallbar?" said a female voice.

"Yes," she said timidly.

"Great, hold one second I am going to put you on the line with our news anchor Phil Jenkins," the voice said without asking what Emma thought of that.

The line came back to life almost instantly, "Emma? Is that you? This is Phil Jenkins you are live on NBC news. We are sorry for the loss of your mother, do you have any idea if your father is alive or dead?"

"No," she said weakly, between sobs. She fell down on her couch. She had no strength left in her legs. Who entire body was shaking, and she suddenly felt cold.

"Can you tell us what it is like to have lost your mother so tragically?" he asked speaking as fast as he could.

"You want to know how it feels?" she asked.

She had expected that to be the question, but now that she heard it she was angrier than she had ever been in her life. She crossed the room, threw open the window, and threw the cell phone out onto the parking lot below.

As she watched it fall fly from the fifth story window she realized there was a crowd in the parking lot. She was worried for a second the falling phone might hit them. That would be one thing too many to deal with emotionally, if she had just hit someone with a phone.

Then it hit her. Everyone in the crowd was holding either a camera or a microphone. Somehow the media had found her. In force…there had to be thirty of them. There was one campus security guard arguing with them about staying away from the door. He was shouting at them to leave campus but they weren't budging.

She was surrounded! Her car was there in the parking lot. She had left it on campus taking a taxi to the airport so she wouldn't have to pay their parking fees. How did they find her?

She didn't exactly hide but how had it been so damn fast?

She sat on the floor with her back to the wall. She could hear questions being shouted at the window. They must have seen her.

She couldn't take it anymore. She started crying. Hysterics took over as she sat on the floor unable to control the emotions running through her brain. She kept thinking of her mother, her friends, her father, and now everyone wanted to talk to her. People she didn't know wanted to have her answer questions. What the hell was going on? Why her?

***

She awoke with a start. She was awakened by a knock at the door. It was 8AM. She must have been asleep for hours. She partially remembered being awake in the early morning hours after midnight, but nightmares were something she did not expect. She should have expected that her mind would invent horrors as she slept, but she wasn't ready for it. They had plagued her in different forms all night.

She went to the door and asked, "Who is it?" hoping it wasn't a news crew.

"Emma, its Doctor Scott, the headmaster," said the person.

She flung the door open glad it was someone friendly, "Doctor, I'm sorry I haven't had a chance to shower, I must look terrible. What can I do for you?" she asked.

"Don't worry about that Emma. I can't imagine what you are going through. I take it you haven't been outside?" he asked.

"No, not since yesterday when I got back here," she said.

"Not to alarm you but there are news media surrounding the building. I came to sneak you out if that's ok with you," he said.

"I saw it yesterday when I threw my cell phone out the window. It kept ringing. I couldn't take it," she said, feeling a little silly for having thrown the thing out the window.

"Well yesterday, as I understand it, there were about thirty. If my estimate is right it is closer to three hundred now," he said.

"Wait, what? Did you say three hundred?" she couldn't believe it. She asked it as she went to the window. They were everywhere. The appeared to have the entire building surrounded. Didn't they realize she didn't even know everything that was happening? What could she possibly tell them that would make a damn difference?

"Sir, I'm not sure I can go out there," she said.

"Emma, I want you to pack a few things. I will go out and put your things in my car. I will then move the car to the door, and park on the grass. I think I can get it within a few feet. You won't have to talk to them if you don't want to. Then I will take you to my house where we have a stone fence around the entire yard and we can keep them away for a while. I'm not sure how long, but it will at least give you a few days before you have to cope with it. Hopefully by then there will be some other story of the week they want to chase," he said calmly.

She guessed that was the best she could do. It then hit her that she never unpacked.

"Well, I never unpacked my suitcase so now is as

good a time as any," she said.

As they made their way downstairs her legs started to shake. With every step she became unsure of herself more and more. He was true to his word and got his car within a few feet of the door. She covered her face and ran out. She made it before they could do more than snap a few photos.

***

It had been two days. The headmaster had been hospitable and had not asked any questions about her parents. She had called the embassy and left contact information so she could be reached after destroying her phone in dramatic fashion, which had been replayed on television for the past two days. She had no idea why a flying cell phone was news. But there it was, circulating every broadcast, website, and social media over and over again.

Every time the phone rang her heart would race. It was always for Dr. Scott or his family, but she held out hope for her father.

Then the call came. Her father had perished when the hotel fell. She was almost relieved. Not knowing was worse than knowing. Then she felt an overwhelming guilt for her feeling of relief.

Now all she had to do was figure out what happened next. She had planned to share news about her future life with her family, but now those plans seemed meaningless. Just thinking about what the holidays were supposed to be like still brought tears to her eyes. She had wanted to share the news about her new direction in life.

Then it hit her. She could make a difference. She could spend her life finding ways to fix things. Some people said climate shifts caused this damn super storm, and they claimed it could be fixed, if only all of the science and engineering could be sorted out. That would be her life goal. She got dressed in the best clothes she had and walked out to the fence of the property where the news crews were still waiting for her to poke her head out.

She had seen her mother do this sort of impromptu unscheduled interview, and from time to time they had cornered her to speak about what it was like to have a mother like hers. She never knew what to say when they asked those questions. She had never had a different mother. She loved the one she had and never thought of what life would be like with anyone else filling that role.

Now she had a plan, she had something to say about solving the global warming problem, and she had the attention that would enable her to get the word out. The climate geeks on the news always seemed to miss that point. They always wanted to talk about who was to blame. They never suggested a well-defined approach toward a solution.

She was dressed in black jeans and her most respectful black top. This was not a day for color. As she stepped outside it was not hard to look tired, she was exhausted. She hoped that might work in her favor and prayed that it didn't backfire to work against her. When her mother did this, she had image consultants. Emma had just herself. She was alone in the world now. She was supposed to have her whole life in front of her and instead it had been shattered.

They had been pointing cameras at the front and rear doors of the house day and night. She had even seen a wide shot of the headmaster's home on the local news. Somehow it was considered news that she was "inside grieving the loss."

She would be seen the moment she stepped outside. She had to do it sooner or later.

Part of her wanted to hide her face and walk away from them as quickly as possible. The other part of her wanted to follow through on her plan. Even standing by the door preparing to emerge, it was hard to tell which part of her would win.

She took a deep breath, gathered her strength, stepped to the door, and the crowd instantly rushed forward.

"Emma! How do you feel? How does it feel to have lost your parents so tragically? Do you think this tragedy could have been prevented?" asked one of them louder than the rest.

Her mother once told her that they really didn't care if you answered what they asked; they were satisfied if you just said something they could use on video. She decided to just say what she wanted, and avoid the topic, mostly, of her parents. There would be a time and a place for that.

"The tragedy in the South Pacific was shared by many people. Remember Tahiti is just one island in a long chain of islands that is still being pummeled by cyclone Cladis.

"Since no one else has said it on the news, we don't know the extent of the damage or how many people have perished. My parents were among them, that much is known, but so are many other parents, sisters, brothers, sons and daughters. It is important to keep our focus on the fact that not just movie stars and wealthy vacationers were harmed," she said managing to keep her voice from breaking with emotion, for the most part.

She held her head up and looked into the camera, "The world is changing. I have been watching, along with everyone, the reports coming from Tahiti. Like everyone else under the age of sixty, I have heard reports of global climate change my entire life. Has it been caused by humans or not…we have all heard it. There are two camps on this. One is that humans have caused climatological changes, and the other is that it is a natural process caused by our Sun or some other non-human phenomenon.

"I, for one, am tired of hearing the argument. I don't care who or what is to blame.

"Climate change has happened, and my parents and friends are dead. My home has been destroyed and may be rendered uninhabitable if this kind of storm becomes the norm instead of some 'once in a millennium' thing. I don't care about the cause. That doesn't matter anymore.

"I would like the world to know that in the name of my mother, my beautiful, intelligent mother and my devastatingly handsome father, I am going to dedicate my life to doing something these scientists and politicians playing the blame game have refused to do. I am going to solve this problem, not just determine who is to blame. I just applied for early graduation from prep school and plan to apply to The University of Arizona. Right now, as I understand it, they are the best equipped in the nation, with the faculty and facilities, to be able to work on a way to save our planet. I am going to be a part of that.

"Thanks for giving me some of your air time," she said, and walked back inside. As soon as she went back inside Doctor Scott was waiting for her. She wasn't sure her legs were going to carry her to the door, but she managed to make it.

"Emma that was very brave of you. Many people refuse to do anything about that subject other than bicker. I firmly believe you will do something about it all. In fact, there is a friend of mine already on the phone for you," he said.

"Hello," she said.

"Hi. I am trying to reach Emma Hallbar," said the male voice.

"This is Emma," she said a little more timidly than she intended.

"I am Professor Westlake, the President of the University of Arizona. First, I want to offer my condolences. How are you holding up? It must seem like the entire world has been trying to reach you," he said.

"Thank you for that. Yes, Doctor Scott has been nice enough to offer me a place to hide," she said gaining confidence.

"I am sorry to bother you in what must be a time of grief, but I saw you on television. According to our records, you have never applied here. However, I want to offer you a place at our University. We have one of the best programs in the nation for the problems you want to solve. I hope you don't mind but I know your headmaster and wanted to see what kind of student you were. Given the problems you face, if you like, you can skip the normal application process and consider yourself in. From what your headmaster said, along with your background and SAT scores, I am sure you will be a welcome member of our student body," he said.

"Professor, I am honored. Thank you so much. I was not looking forward to the application process. I want you to know I won't let you down," she said speaking very quickly. She thought that this special treatment was probably because of her mother, but she didn't really care at that moment.

"I'm sure you won't. I am going to have my assistant contact you to handle the particulars, and we look forward to seeing you when you are ready. I recommend you not start in the coming semester, but rather wait for the fall. Take some time to heal, not to mention to handle everything needed to get your personal affairs in order. I can't imagine what you are going through, but if I can do anything, please reach out," he said. He gave her his personal contact information, not just his office information.

When she hung up the only thing she could think of was that she no longer had a cellular phone of her own.

"Doctor Scott, can you take me to my car or to a cellular store? I kind of need to replace my phone. I destroyed it the other day," she said thinking that it was time to at least leave the house.

"Certainly, I will gladly go with you in case they bother you anymore," he said pointing to the media crews as he spoke.

Chapter Four

Emma couldn't understand how it had all occurred. Suddenly she was being referred to as a celebrity. People would follow her with cameras, people she didn't know would ask to get their picture taken with her. Something about the combination of the video of her mom and her impromptu press conference outside the headmaster's house had thrust her into the spotlight, and it didn't seem to be dimming.

One or two of her mother's friends from Hollywood helped her find a way through the shark-infested waters of massive public scrutiny. She had a lot to remember. There was a whole "celebrity" image to keep now. She needed help with clothing, makeup, how to stand, hairstyles, and anything else that would help her get her message out, if she wanted to bring focus to the problem of how to put an end to climate change. She hated it all. She thought her message should be enough, but that wasn't the way the world worked. She had to be liked, and much to her chagrin, the public image mattered. She did it, but she didn't like it.

Solutions were needed, and only some kind of focal point was going to make that possible. It was nice to see her mother's friends, it made her feel like she had some surrogate parents to turn to for advice. The loss had been horrific, she still had nightmares, but having someone older to talk to helped considerably.

The headmaster explained to her that public image

done properly could amplify a message massively. It could make an idea have a life of its own, and therefore a possible longshot solution could find some support.

Her public image was never something she thought about. Right after her first, and what she had assumed what would be her only, appearance on television, people said they liked her. She had assumed it was a purely sympathetic reaction to her personal loss and grief. Sooner or later, if she was going to stay in the public eye, that sympathy would go away.

Emma didn't care about being famous, in fact she really despised the fact that she would have to use her name to get something done. On the other hand, she did want to solve the problem so that no one else would lose their loved ones in the same fashion she did.

Being famous did take some getting used too. In the blink of an eye she went from no one thinking her opinion was more than that of any other high school senior, to people seeking her opinion on subjects that had global implications. She was the same person, she hated the fact that she had cameras pointed at her all the time. There were days when a woman really doesn't want to be photographed. There was even a time when someone was paying a huge bounty for a picture of her without makeup.

She had more concerns than the public scrutiny and internet fame to cope with. After the passing of her parents, there was an estate to deal with. She was their only child so it all came to her, but the amount of money coming in and going out staggered her mind. Her old budget was measured in hundreds of dollars a month, but now nothing managed to fall in her lap with amounts below a few thousand dollars, and sometimes much more. She was also shocked when she found out how much money her mother had saved. She turned to some of her mother's friends who got her in front of a professional money manager who put all of her assets into a trust.

It was a large shift in her thinking. Suddenly she had to learn to manage money, and she had to deal with people following her with cameras to take her picture doing everything from grocery shopping to exercising. There were days she just wanted the world to go away so she could cry. Her parents were dead, she had no one. Her grandparents had been gone for years. There were no brothers, sisters, cousins, or even a boyfriend to turn to. She constantly felt alone with all of these cameras pointed at her. All of these people wanting to have a photograph, and she felt alone. It was almost too much to deal with.

For weeks she had been numb, emotionally and physically. She realized she had enough credits to graduate early, so that was just what she did.

She took that time to start reading everything she could on the subject of climate change. Some of it good, some of it bad, some of it easily discredited, but she read as much of it as she could.

She discovered that there were natural shifts that

were reasonably well understood. The earth had undergone multiple ice ages, warm periods, and everything in between. There was also a huge controversy over modern day shifts being faster than those found historically. Those shifts, it was believed by some, were caused by mankind. She wasn't sure she believed that was possible, but she believed that the climate was shifting. If it was natural or manmade she didn't know and didn't care. All she wanted was to find out if it could be prevented. With all of the advanced scientific knowledge available to mankind she wanted to find a way to put a stop to it. Who was to blame could be problem for someone else.

There were so many people acting as experts who were clearly misinformed on the subject that it created widespread controversy. She had this new public image, and some connections in Hollywood. She decided to work on a group of short video clips for her YouTube Channel.

She made sure these videos were in layperson's language, as she was barely more than a layperson herself. Her whole point was to try to set the record straight for those people who had not read much on the subject, and tended to present themselves as experts spreading clearly false information. She brought in other video co-stars with recognizable names in entertainment and science, and gathered quite a following in very little time.

There were groups who said the world had to stop emitting carbon immediately, which meant stopping the burning of fossil fuels. That was not ever going to happen in a meaningful way as far as she could tell.

There was a small, relatively unheard group that were trying to find a way to make it so that mankind could maintain their lifestyle and keep the climate stable. In one video she referred to this as the Holy Grail of climate technology. That was where she wanted to focus her career. The Holy Grail may not exist, she might not ever find it, but she had to try.

The videos ended up having an impact. The second was that people started thinking of climate change differently. Now there were discussions that went beyond assigning blame. People started discussing rational solutions.

Once in a while someone would reach out and tell her she was wrong. Normally they would not be terribly polite, but that was the gist of the incoming message. One person said that climate change was just an invention of the media designed to get ratings. She immediately went to work on that person. She didn't expect to get them all to believe in what she was trying to do, but she would try.

All of the public attention made her understand why her mother preferred to stay as far from Hollywood as she could when she wasn't working. Her mom wanted to be an actress, not a celebrity. So often people confused those two.

Emma started getting invitations to more social functions than she could possibly ever attend. It forced her to become strategic in choosing which ones to say yes to. She would find out who was going, and if there was someone there who could help her expand the concept of fixing the problem rather than assigning blame, off she went.

It took her a few months to summon the strength, but she finally decided it was time to visit Tahiti. She naively tried to just buy an airline ticket. It turned out all commercial airlines had ceased services to the island. It was no longer profitable because almost no one wanted to travel there, according to a travel agent she talked to on the phone.

She looked into how close she could get using publicly available transportation, and it wasn't very close at all. She was in California visiting a friend of her mother's while she attempted to make the arrangements. It was so frustrating that she vented about how challenging it was just to go home because the storm had destroyed the popularity of Tahiti as a tourist destination. She was surprised to learn that the friend owned a luxury private jet and offered to fly her there.

She never gave much thought to the affluence of some of the people she knew because of her mother's chosen career. She would never ask someone for such a favor, but in this case she jumped at the unsolicited offer.

Her friend was an experienced public personality, and she had a thought.

This could be more than just a trip home. This visit could help people see through the eyes of a native Tahitian what that storm had done. Why fly a jet all the way there for just her? Why not use some of the extra seats that would be available and make the most of the trip.

She got in contact with Stephanie Verum, a well-known documentary filmmaker who had done a special on the island starring her mother years before. Some documentary footage of the current conditions on the island could help her crusade to raise public awareness. Emma was flattered that Stephanie wanted her to be the on-camera host for a new film. Once finished it would be an hour-long television special.

Before leaving California, they collected some interview footage for the documentary. She answered questions about what it was like growing up on the island and how it felt to watch as the news broke. She even answered questions, for the first time since everything happened, about her mother and her untimely, and very graphic passing, something she had yet to do publicly.

They gathered a camera crew that was experienced in fieldwork, added a survivalist just in case, and obtained all of the equipment and supplies they would need for a few days. It took a few weeks to prepare, but they managed to get everything together and scheduled the trip to allow her to return to the States in time to start her first semester at the University.

As they neared the island, she found herself getting nervous. She had seen the video and satellite imagery other people had put on the news, but for some reason she didn't want to believe what she had seen. She preferred to believe that only exceptionally dramatic shots had been used to attract an audience through sensationalism. She hoped that the entire island wasn't as bad as what she had seen.

She was hoping with every fiber of her being that this trip would reveal that the damage was merely overhyped by the media. Then she could visit, take some video, perhaps bring a few things back as mementos, and move on with life. She was scheduled to start classes at the University of Arizona in two weeks, and she needed achieve some level of closure.

As they came in for a landing, she sat as far from the windows as she could. She knew that looking from the air and assessing the level of damage would only make her upset due to seeing the entire storm aftermath at once. She wanted to take baby steps and see it in small doses. The documentary crew also thought that would be better for their purposes. They wanted to capture her first reaction to different locations of the island, not a second, less emotional response.

They taxied to the end of the runway and the first thing she noticed was that they were not pulling up to the airport terminal. They weren't even close to it. She asked the pilot, "Why are we parking out here and not near the building?"

"We received word from ground control that the building is being condemned. They are asking all inbound traffic to park in various taxiway locations and to be met by shuttles. In your case we managed to get your transportation inside the fence, so we won't have to shuttle you to your cars, and they are just going to let you load all your luggage and gear right into the trucks," he said.

"Trucks? We certainly don't need trucks, why not just a regular car, you know, something simple?" she wondered aloud.

"I asked for the trucks," their survivalist, a retired Navy SEAL named Jacobs said.

"Why?" she asked innocently.

"I did some checking and very few roads are still intact. We may need the trucks to get to places you want to go, and I didn't want to take any chances on getting stuck someplace," he said.

She walked down the steps of the gantry and breathed in the salt air for the first time in almost a year. Something was different. She grew up here and instantly knew that the air was just not right. It was supposed to be salty yet filled with the scent of all of the flowers indigenous to the island. The smell that she encountered was quite different from what she remembered. She assumed it was because she was near the jet engines that had just shut down, but it smelled awful. Perhaps it was just the way the airport smelled outside right next to the runway? She shrugged it off as nothing, and reminded herself that she had never deplaned outside, instead of directly into a terminal. Maybe it was because she had just been gone too long.

She looked at the terminal building and saw that all of the windows were blown out. Some had been replaced with plywood, but some still appeared to be ghostly eyes peering out from a destroyed building. She could see ceiling tiles lying around and wires dangling in all directions, but absolutely no sign of life inside. If she watched closely she could see a bird fly out every once in a while. In each case it came out of the building so quickly that it looked like some supernatural apparition was chasing it.

She knew that the camera would be rolling the entire time they were on the ground in order capture her first impressions of the island. They had even done her hair, makeup and wardrobe before landing for her homecoming to look just right on video. She had her long hair tied back, minimal makeup, jeans, a white t-shirt, and hiking boots. This was a day for rugged clothing. If any surprises occurred, the continuous video recordings would capture it.

She had been asked to talk about how she felt as she noticed things. They would edit out anything that wasn't interesting later. "My first impression as I got off the plane was that the air is salty just like I expected, but there was also a smell that I can't place. My guess is that it was because we deplaned on the taxiway, and there is always going to be a jet engine smell there.

"As I look around, I can't see much from here except the airport building. Many of the windows are boarded up. Those that aren't covered with wood are just holes with some pieces of shattered glass still stuck in the frames that makes it look like they have jagged teeth or something. It is really upsetting to think that just a few months ago this airport was so inviting to so many people. Back then it gave an amazing first impression of the paradise one would expect from Tahiti.

"The building does not look like anyone has been

inside to clean it up in all the months since the disaster. The pilot told us that the building has been condemned and as I look at it, knocking it down and rebuilding from scratch might be the easiest solution. There are even electric wires dangling from the ceiling, but not a single electric light on anyplace, and it looks unsafe to turn on the power. I guess that with no tourism industry remaining, they chose not to focus on this area, and worry more about basic services for the permanent island residents. We are going to make our way to where my parents and I lived, in an area known as Afaahiti," she said hoping they could edit her dialogue if she sounded incoherent or rambled too much without making the end product appear to have been staged.

They rode along in silence through the airport grounds. They stopped by the airport exit as someone flagged them down.

"Hey, are you our guide?" Jacobs asked out the window.

"Yes, I am Paul. I was sent by the local governor to make sure you avoid getting hurt. Not much is open yet I am afraid, so let's try to get you through this intact. Do you have enough bottled water?" he asked. "We don't have a reliable water supply in this area yet."

"We should have enough consumables for a few days," replied Jacobs.

Emma was shocked by that. She had expected at least basic services to be functional everywhere. It had been months. Why couldn't they have running water back up and functional everywhere?

When they came out and she saw the roadway, she gasped. The level of destruction was amazing. Roads were washed away. Where there used to be fields of lush flora, now there were piles of wreckage from what remained of various buildings and homes.

She struggled to keep her emotions under control as she spoke. "I remember many of these fields as open land. Some of them were farmland for crops like vanilla and fruits. I hope someplace they are still growing those things. If they don't, there won't be much of an economy left here at all. Most of our economy on Tahiti had been based on tourism, but there were always a few farmers. Most people live close to the water, so I suppose they had to stack up the destroyed houses someplace while they thought about what to do with them," she said for the camera.

She looked closer for any signs of life. She didn't see anything moving but them. She couldn't even find signs of much wildlife except for the occasionally bird.

"Paul, I don't see anyone anywhere, where is everyone living?"

"There are a few towns still inhabitable but not many. Most people have left the island. We are still trying to do some reconstruction, but after the vast majority of the economy was destroyed, things became very expensive. It was so bad that at one point a hamburger was a full day of minimum wage salary. As a result, once the relief supplies started to slow down, people found their way off the island," he said.

"How many people still live here?" she asked.

"Our population is about 10% of what it was before the storm. So many people were killed that not a lot of people wanted to stay. Remember we lost 23% of our population in one day. There were five giant waves that came in with absolutely no warning. The largest of them measured almost 40 meters high when it hit the shore. I'm not sure I believe that measurement, but I wasn't here. I was on Hawaii at the time, although this is where I was born. Right now things are so bad from a basic services perspective that unless you are part of the rebuilding effort we are asking people to leave…temporarily," he said.

"When did you go to school here?" she asked.

"I was two years in front of you," he said.

"I thought you looked familiar. Did you work at my father's hotel for a while?" she asked.

"One summer. I parked cars. We actually had a long conversation once. I think I annoyed you asking too many questions about one of your older friends. That was back when you used to sit in the garden there and study, I think it was the year before you left for the prep school back in the United States," he said.

"I remember that," she said, glad she could finally place him and connect with anything from her youth. Part of her had been afraid her entire life had been erased.

They turned the corner and she saw the road that ran along the beach to where the hotel had been. She expected to see the well-paved road that had always been there along with grass and palm trees to one side with ocean on the other. What they found was a road cracked apart into fragments with weeds growing out of it. It looked like it had been abandoned for years. She even saw parts of a boat sitting in the middle of what she would charitably call the road.

Paul leaned over to the driver, "Drive off the road to the right side. The dirt is actually better to drive on than the concrete at this point. If you try to stay on that you will probably lose a tire."

Emma looked out the window and saw something she never would have imagined. It looked like something out of World War II documentaries. The concrete was in pieces with rebar reinforcement rods sticking up at odd directions. It was obvious they *would* lose a tire, or worse, by staying on the roads. Nothing she remembered was anywhere to be seen. There weren't even crews of workmen clearing things away. She briefly thought of Hiroshima, and then shook her head to clear the image from her mind.

"Why aren't any cleanup crews working?" she asked.

"This kind of destruction is actually pretty minimal compared to most of the island. Here the wave hit and carried everything off. In other areas the weather hit and just blew things around. They are pretty busy over at the port trying to get that back up and running. Being able to get supplies in without any issues has to be our priority. There has been some discussion of abandoning the island. Remember we not only got hit by *Cladis* but we have had two other pretty major storms since then. Every time we start getting things cleaned up, it gets all messed up again," Paul explained.

The world had been so focused on the super storm that they had ignored the minor storms that hampered the cleanup effort since that time. She was upset with herself for not thinking about what had happened since *Cladis*.

It was Jacobs' turn to make her feel worse, and she had been starting to think that wasn't possible. "How bad has the looting been?" he asked.

"Pretty bad actually. We have had to start carrying handguns when traveling alone. There is usually safety in numbers, but desperate people do desperate things," Paul explained.

They drove on in silence. She couldn't believe that the people she grew up with would resort to that. Everyone here helped everyone. This wasn't her home, this was some type of hell on Earth.

They came around the bend and there it was. The hotel that used to be her home. The road going up to it was gone. It was all tall grass. It looked like nobody had been here since they pulled out the bodies.

They managed to drive within a few hundred yards. "From here we should walk," Jacobs said. She got out and stood on the ground she used to jog along while enjoying the sunrise.

"Well, this used to be home," she said to the camera.

They followed her as she followed Jacobs along the path up to the building that was lying over on its side. It just hit her that the smell had not gone away.

"Paul, I'm used to the salt air but there is something new. It isn't fish, it isn't jet fumes. what is it? It's new and everywhere?" she asked.

"Ummmm," Paul stammered.

Jacobs spoke up, "That's dead bodies. There is no mistaking the smell. They have been there a while so it isn't as bad as it once was I'm sure," he said.

"What?!" she exclaimed, stopping in her tracks.

"With the amount of destruction there was just no way, not enough crews and equipment to pull everyone out. There is so much stuff on top of some of the bodies it hasn't been safe to get in there without heavy equipment to try to recover everything from all over the island," Paul explained.

"How many people are still unaccounted for," she screamed at their guide. Her heart was beating so fast she thought it was going to fly out of her chest.

"A few thousand. Some were probably taken out to sea but some are still inside structures including the hotel here," he said.

She fell to her knees. Tears were coming down her cheeks. Her entire body was shaking. She hadn't felt like this since that first day in her dorm room. She felt like she was going to throw up. She didn't even care if the cameras caught it.

"You mean the place I used to call home is now a tomb but we don't know to how many people or who they are?" she asked between sobs.

No one answered. They didn't need to.

"Take me back to the airport, I can't do this. I wanted to, but I just can't go further," she said.

On the drive back to the airport she apologized to the documentary crew. They said it was fine. They would take her back to the plane, then go out for a few hours and get some footage of different areas. She agreed instantly as long as she didn't have to go. She waited on the plane thinking about what had happened. She had more that she wanted to say.

Once they were back in the air, after just a few hours on the ground, she asked them to turn on the camera and record something.

She looked directly into the camera, "I know people will say that mankind didn't do this. Maybe they are right, maybe they aren't, but mankind can fix it. We can make these storms a thing of the past and we must. We must at least make an attempt before it is too late for any of us," she said.

She fell asleep from stress shortly after that, and did not wake up until they landed in Los Angeles.

Chapter Five

"The two most important days in your life are the day you were born, and the day you discover the reason you were born." – Mark Twain

After the loss of her family, and witnessing, first hand, that her former home had been turned into a tomb, Emma had fallen into a deep depression. There were days when she couldn't find it within herself to get out of bed.

She had been ready to drop out of school, not going to University at all, and become a recluse. At least then she could never suffer loss again. Being alone sounded like the perfect plan. She could avoid the cameras, she could avoid television, and mostly never feel close enough to anything just to have it ripped away from her again.

Some friends of her parents sat her down and convinced her to spend at least one semester in school. To "throw herself into her schoolwork," in their words, and perhaps having a new place, new friends, and a new direction in life would help her find ways to not continually relive these constant feelings of loss. They claimed that being alone would have the exact opposite effect from what she wanted. Emma didn't care. She wanted no attachments, but in the end, decided to give it one semester. She decided she could go to class, sit in the back, and not interact with anyone unless it was absolutely necessary.

After getting a few weeks into the semester she found that the more she worked, the less she had time to think about her parents. It even reduced the number of nightmares. Finally they reduced in number to once a week, rather than the twice a night they had been poking their heads into her subconscious.

Even before visiting Tahiti, she had this nightly recurring dream about being on the island as the storm hit and watching, helplessly, screaming, and struggling to save her parents as they both perished. After the trip, which she now regretted, the dreams included many of the people she knew, and some people she would have recognized but couldn't claim credit to know, like her pharmacist, or the old lady who sold flowers. But they weren't the people as she had known them. They were half-rotted zombie versions, of their former selves.

She did her one semester, and then decided to stick around at school, and even increased her semester loads. She took every class possible that could be squeezed into her schedule with every new semester. She even went to school on the short semesters offered over holidays and summers.

She quickly discovered that there were national and international conferences on the subject of climate change and managed to find her way to as many of those as her hectic course load would allow. She kept meticulous notes, she networked with scientists already working in the field, and drove herself to work harder with the notion that somewhere in this already completed body of work was the answer, if you merely assembled all of the parts in the right order.

One Sunday afternoon she found herself free of those dreaded exams. She had a spare day off with nothing to study. She took the time to clean out her dorm room and thought she might call a friend to go to a movie, and suddenly realized her roster of friends was essentially nonexistent. Sure, there were people from class or from research but they weren't friends. That had originally been by design, and she thought maybe it was nearly time to change that, but she wasn't ready yet.

Semesters came and went. She made very few friends, but she built an amazing professional network. She was asked out on dates from time to time by men she met around campus. She even went sometimes, but there was only one thing she was serious about, and that was graduating as fast as possible.

Some part of her missed having a social life, but only a small part. She felt good about being a part of something greater than herself, and working on the future of the climate was something that could be greater than any living human. She never entered into the discussions on the causes of climate change, those were secondary. She only wanted to solve it, to stabilize the environment for all time. She was certain there had to be a way. If the mechanisms for change were fully understood, then a solution could be found by "dialing the right scientific knobs," as one of her professors put it.

She managed to complete the undergraduate program and earn a degree in a quick three years giving her degrees in Mathematics and Astronomy.

The very next day after the graduation ceremony was over, she went to the campus bookstore to buy the required texts for the first semester of graduate work. She managed to finish her coursework as well as dissertations and required qualifying exams to be awarded a PhD in the absolute minimum time possible. The professors in the department couldn't believe how fast it was, but she was the most dedicated student they had ever seen.

When asked about why the rush, all Emma could say was that she wanted to get out of the classroom and get to work. The awesome impact that global warming and the ensuing climate change was having would not wait for her.

While she was a student, she had attended and participated in a large number of conferences. For some reason that eluded and annoyed her, the media had decided that she needed to be followed. They followed the daughter of the famous actress on her quest. Apparently they found her focus area for her research controversial, and that meant viewers. Viewers meant ratings and increased advertising revenue. She didn't really care as long as she got to do the work she wanted to do. She did occasionally try to avoid them, but there was always that pesky voice in the back of her brain that said her being well known for doing this kind of work might come in handy if she needed favors. She played the game a little, but it seemed like the more she resisted, the more people wanted to know where she was, and what she was doing 24 hours a day.

In her last two years of graduate school, as her work matured, her presentations became media events. Whoever saw the broadcasts heard about how the Earth's atmosphere was in a state of chaos. Based on the number of potential inputs that created the current state of the atmosphere at any given time, her contention had always been that identifying the cause was difficult and wasn't as important as solving the problem. People also heard, most of them for the first time that solutions existed to stop the madness.

She had become so well known that she had somehow managed to attract attention of many non-scientists. People from all walks of life offered moral support. That actually meant a lot to her. She really felt that these were the kinds of people she wanted to help. She felt like she didn't want to get to know these people so well that she felt their losses, but she did want to protect them. Someone had to stop the tragedies and save lives.

During one very large presentation some protestors managed to get in the room and start calling her a fraud. They went on to say she was just trying to capitalize on her parent's misfortune for her own profit. She didn't understand that because so far she had spent a ton of money on school and not even landed a job, but why should a little dose of reality got in the way of a good protest.

The protestors really bothered her for a few days. She finally managed to console herself with the fact that she would save those people along with everyone else if she could figure out how to fix things. They may disagree with her, or maybe they just wanted to get their 15 minutes of fame, but they would be safe nonetheless.

During her time as a student, in the few periods of time she wasn't studying, she started a non-profit fund in her parent's name. She donated some money herself from her inheritance, and managed to raise some money through her mother's contacts with only one goal: to raise public awareness on how the problem of climate change could be fixed.

She would freely admit, and had said many times publicly, that she was not the most brilliant person working in her field. But most people would say that she was the hardest working.

Scientists rarely had problems explaining their work in a way that people in their field would understand, and those scientists working outside their field might marginally be able to follow. Emma seemed to have a unique ability to make anyone, from any walk of life who would give her a chance, understand her work, and make them feel like it needed to be supported.

In recent months she started facing a new, and somewhat unexpected challenge. The more well-known she became, the more there was an increasing social component to her job. For many of the meetings, especially those in Washington DC, many people brought their spouses or significant others. She had no such person in her life, and at these events it was horribly obvious that she was single. That led many people to attempt to play matchmaker, which was annoying. She dealt with it politely, but viewed those occurrences as a waste of time.

Those conferences, and trips to Washington DC were a necessary evil. Her plan to fix things was simple. It involved some well-understood science and engineering. She found a way to make the system simple enough that it should be able to meet all of the goals she had for climate control. The problem was so complex to discuss that the solution had to be simple, or no one would take the risk of building the system, especially given that it was going to be one of the most expensive engineering projects of all time.

Conceptually it was simple. Merely block some of the light coming from the sun. If that could be done, it would reduce the overall amount of energy coming into the atmosphere, and as a result reduce warming, and if done properly could stabilize the climate. The details were a bit more complex than that, but she managed to convince anyone who would listen that it could be done. She had once described it as putting sunglasses on the earth.

Emma had explained the solution so many times she probably could have done it in her sleep. It was kind of annoying because she had done it on camera so often, and those videos had been watched so many times, that she often thought people just wanted to hear her repeat it so they could say she told them directly. It really bothered her, but she did it anyway.

It involved the well-known scientific principles of satellite orbits. With proper use, that knowledge base would allow the shading of sunlight. She had examined a series of increasingly higher orbits until she found one that could hold the sunshades that she thought should be built in position with a minimum of station-keeping assistance. That station keeping would require motors, and motors would require fuel. The less fuel that could be used would mean a reduced cost of operation.

The entire concept was based on the fact that at a distance four times further from the surface of the Earth than the moon was the orbit Emma wanted. The architecture she had come up with depended on it. This spot in space is known within scientific communities as the Sun-Earth Lagrange Point L1.

The beauty that arose from the simplicity of the sunshades being placed at this Lagrange Point first came to her attention in her undergraduate years. Lagrange points could be calculated from the physical laws and mathematics known to Isaac Newton centuries ago. There was nothing to invent, all that had to be done was implement everything on a scale much larger than ever before done.

She reflected on the plans she had formulated as a PhD candidate while she applied her makeup in preparation for a Washington DC cocktail party. A party at which she would explain her plan all over again, and then again after that. Repetition was necessary and she didn't mind, as long as she was gaining more support for the project.

She wanted to make sure the concept became reality. This wasn't just a quest for a degree or some peer reviewed papers, or even tenure at a university, this was a quest to preserve the planet as a place humans could inhabit. She knew that tonight people would be using her formal title and it would take her a while to get used to being called doctor, but it was now official. She had her degree and now she wanted to put it to use.

Dr. Emma Hallbar was going to work. Hopefully tonight she could get more of the right people on her side, and take one more step toward making the dream a reality.

Chapter Six

Andrew A. Smith entered the room and was immediately struck by the security precautions being taken. Even for a government building they were intense. The invitation had reached him through his corporation's lobbying firm, and it was clear from the start that it was not an invitation he should refuse.

Andy Smith was the CEO of a company with very strong ties to the government. He had never heard of this installation, but the government had lots of facilities all over the globe. It was impossible to keep track of them all. Now that he thought about it, this could be the first time in a long time he attended an event without knowing who sent him the invitation.

As the CEO of an energy corporation with global reach, he was responsible for providing a significant percentage of all of the energy consumed in the United States.

Once he cleared security he began to relax a little. As the reception area started to fill, he sipped the coffee he had been handed by one of the roaming waiters and started to recognize a few people. There were other CEOs, some of which he had met personally, or knew by reputation. Andy had never seen a collection of power at this level in one room, all at the same time.

Someone opened a door that had been guarded by two conspicuous security guards. Then the announcement came, "Ladies and Gentlemen, The

President of the United States."

Andy scrambled to his feet with the rest of the astonished group. He recognized the Speaker of the House and a few of the other political leaders who joined the President at a massive mahogany table centered on the stage.

"Ladies and Gentlemen, I want to extend my personal thanks, and the thanks of your nation, for joining us here today," the President said. "The results of this meeting will positively influence the future of our country as an economic power. We will need help from every one of you to achieve the goal of retaining a leadership position in world affairs, which in the near future will be in a state of turmoil. I cannot overstate the importance of the role each of you is being asked to play.

"Without discussing the details, a controlling faction within the legislative branch of our government has made it clear that in the wake of the weather-related tragedies and sea level rise we are now experiencing, the people of our country demand, and will receive, definitive action intended to bring global warming and climate change under control. If we cannot agree here and now on a constructive way forward, another way forward will happen without us; a way that effectively bans the use of fossil fuels, even though the rest of the world would not be legally obligated to follow suit, and so the effective impact of this policy on global climate would almost certainly be insufficient."

"Each of you controls a company that is responsible for a significant segment of our economy in this country. More specifically, a segment that is under threat if fossil fuels are eliminated from our portfolio of energy sources. The economic, and hence political and military, worldwide leadership position of our country is at stake."

"We have identified an approach to fix these climate problems that does not require curtailing fossil fuel use at all. It also, potentially, enables global climate control by the actions of our country alone. The global nature of it will however require United Nations participation so that the rest of the world feels included in decisions about managing our planet. They won't necessarily be involved in the solution, but we have to at least make them feel as though they are."

"Congressman Fox, Chairman of the Congressional Committee on the Environment, will now explain this plan in a general way with just enough detail for you to appreciate that it preserves all of your current business operations. In fact, some of you will benefit from contracts related to the construction of the solution. Your political support for this program is essential, in my opinion, and also in the opinions of those you see before you, to the future of this country. We will need your help to ensure the votes are obtained in the legislature to get what we are going to propose through without a hiccup."

***

Emma had explained the idea for the ultimate

climate control system so many times, to people of all levels of scientific and engineering backgrounds, that she was fairly confident she could do it in her sleep. She had discussed it on television, at conferences, while defending her dissertation, and even once to some random person in a hotel bar who merely asked what she did for a living.

She knew she would do it again, as many times as she had to until it became a reality. She didn't mind. This was a small price to pay if she could reach the goal of controlling the climate shifts that were killing people. Whether she had to control mankind, or Mother Nature, she really didn't care. Control could be achieved, if people wanted it badly enough.

She knew what the night would be like. She would have to explain her plan over and over again to people, only this time while wearing high heels, and holding a cocktail she wasn't going to drink. Yes, it was another of the all-important social events where she could make connections that could lead to an opportunity to step an inch closer to her ultimate goal.

She knew the person organizing the evening event. The guest list included some very influential decision makers who could push a project the size of what she wanted to do across the finish line, at least from the funding perspective. There were several she wanted to meet, but one in particular she knew that she must.

Her big target was the Chairman of the Congressional Committee on the Environment. If she could get him to believe in the fix, and not allow herself to get sucked into a discussion on the causes of the climate shifts, this could be a big night.

She ran through her arguments to use with him in her head. She reminded herself to avoid the phrase, "save the planet." The planet would survive even if humans did not. People who used such phrases were quickly dismissed as extreme, and she wasn't that. She just wanted to help other people not suffer a loss similar to her own. Every single time she thought about her parents she started to feel depressed, or worse nauseated. It was true that if no action was taken mankind could be in jeopardy, and that was the message. The loss of productivity, the loss of capital, the disaster for the economy if no action was taken was where to focus. The remainder of the discussion was a feasibility argument about the technology to do the job.

As she arrived she saw a reception area with hors d'oeuvres setup on tables to one side as well as waiters floating around with additional food items and glasses of wine. There was an additional table with coffee and tea just inside the entry. There were high top tables in the center for people to rest their food and drinks as they talked. There were lower tables with chairs near the back if your discussion required note taking.

The room was crowded. So far she had told her entire project pitch from start to finish twice. The decision to move to Washington after graduate school had been specifically to be close to decision makers. Thanks to all of the conferences and television appearances she had made, she was one of the people that everyone wanted to speak to at these events. That was a double-edged sword. Many people wanted to get their pictures taken with her, and even decision makers wanted to meet, if only for a moment.

One of the problems with events like this and being single at the same time was that everyone noticed you were alone, while everyone else was with a significant other of some sort. She didn't mind being single, but had already had to politely turn down three people trying to set her up in a conversation, and ultimately a date, with "the perfect man." She wasn't sure how everyone else seemed to know who the perfect man was, she wasn't sure what she wanted in a man at this stage of her life. She really didn't even want a serious relationship. She had no clue why people insisted on doing this and explaining to her that it was "for her own good."

She scanned the room looking for the Congressman, hoping he actually came and didn't avoid the evening's festivities. After several minutes of scanning, and rescanning, she found him. She started working her way through the crowd avoiding getting pulled into a conversation. She hovered near him and his staff while he spoke to a group of people, until she could find an opening in the conversation. One of the very few perks of being a somewhat well-known scientist, and daughter of a very well-known actress, was that people would often interrupt what they were doing to take the opportunity to talk to her.

"Congressman Fox, I am Doctor Emma Hallbar. I'm

the one who," she said while holding out her hand.

He cut her off mid-sentence, "I know exactly who you are Doctor. There aren't many people around who don't. You have managed to make a real name for yourself. In a way you managed to help make science popular once again. You seem to have found a way to be on television talking about your plan more than any other scientist I can remember. While people are often intrigued by science and scientists, you somehow make people want to *be* you. Hopefully we won't have any trouble recruiting the next generation of great thinkers into various scientific disciplines. Someone on my staff thinks that you are going to stop doing anything meaningful and just turn into another talking head, but you keep surprising us by doing things that matter, at least at a laboratory scale. Do you think all of your work can really be translated into global scale solutions?"

"Thank you, Mr. Congressman, you flatter me," she said, honestly. His mini speech caught her off guard and excited her all at the same time. She thought she would have to start from scratch and do a hard sell. She was going to try to turn the tables, "Why do you think it can't be done at a global level given the results we have achieved already?"

"Mostly, like most things in this town, it comes down to money. I know what you want to do is going to be costly. I also know you have put out a cost number that makes it sound like it can be sort of achieved. I also know that the early cost estimates on any project this large are almost always off, and usually low. How can we justify the cost overruns that will result in what has to be one of the most costly projects ever attempted?"

"Well Mr. Congressman, I hate to sound like a television soundbite, but fixing any problem of this magnitude, that has been left unchecked for so many years, will be costly. It won't be fixed overnight. In order to justify it we have to examine the cost of doing nothing, which is what we have done so far. Let me offer an analogy. If the problem we are trying to solve is that the engine in your car has seized, then you have to weigh the costs of repairing versus replacing it. When it comes to replacing the Earth's climate, even if the shifts are caused by some natural process, we really can't do that. So, we are left with no alternative but doing the repair. Are you with me so far?" she asked, hoping she wasn't talking too quickly, as she tended to do when she got excited.

"I'm tracking so far. I also agree that we can't attempt to replace the atmosphere, or climate, however you want to phrase it. I also know that having just one solution you are pushing is far from exhaustive of alternative answers. Surely, just because you have one counterargument doesn't mean that there are no alternatives," he said hitting her with a similar argument that so many before her had tried.

"Oh, of course there are alternatives. Let's go through the leaders of the pack. Some people have advocated for a long time, and very vocally, that we merely limit the emissions of fossil fuels through regulation. What those same people always somehow conveniently manage to forget is that we are but one nation. Unless you get all of the nations of the planet to do the same thing that solution will never work, at least not enough to fully solve the problem.

"Then there have been some scientists who have advocated that we should terraform Mars," she said taking a deep breath. "That is an option, Mars can sustain an atmosphere. The question is, how much would that cost. It would take decades after we got started before there was a breathable atmosphere, assuming everything went according to plan, and we aren't even on the surface of the planet with a single human yet," she said.

"Continue," he said nonchalantly indicating he was not yet convinced.

"Then there is the human cost of how many people will suffer or die from extreme weather while we mess around with this other planet. Then there is the question of the cost to relocate some reasonable fraction of the human population all the way to Mars. If we were to move even one billion or so people the cost would exceed the total amount of wealth on the planet. Then there is the fact that this is a death sentence for the majority of the population, all the while we ask that part of the human race to pay for the rest of the global population to move on and survive. Then, how do you decide which people go and who stays? Indeed there have been other proposals, and even other repair proposals, but looking at those alternatives that are viable, I am the cheapest game in town," she said with a grin.

"So, you are telling me, that after a decade or so of

your time and energy you are convinced that the only real option is to do a repair job. I agree with you in that we can't move the entire population of the Earth to some other planet, which is the stuff of science fiction novels. But then, you are also telling me that your version of a repair job is the best course of action. How can you be so sure? If I bring in five other scientists with atmospheric fixes won't they tell me the same thing about their plan, while trashing yours?" he asked.

She had run into this one before as well, "In my dissertation research I have quantitatively compared every single published proposed solution versus the one I am advocating. I have compared them based on effectiveness, cost, and schedule. There relatively inexpensive proposals to reduce the amount of sunlight that reaches the ground by injecting particles into the atmosphere. However, that approach is not controllable in real time like mine. Without control we invite disaster. My work has been peer reviewed many times, and presented to hundreds of scientists at conferences, and read by thousands more in journals. Not one time has anyone disagreed with my reasoning. I think that if you ask a number of climatologists you will find that there is a consensus for the sunshade program," she concluded.

"You are saying, if you will permit me to paraphrase, that your solution is the easiest, cheapest, and the most viable option to save the environment. What about those who say that this is just a personal quest to make yourself feel better after the loss of your parents?" he asked.

She had heard that he liked to get to the heart of matters quickly. That didn't mean that any of those who heard what he said were staring at her any less. Most people just assumed this sort of comment would evoke an emotional response. She had long since learned to hide emotions when it came to her parents, those feelings were hers and hers alone. If she allowed them to become known, people would start to take pity on her again and that would cause her to get depressed even more than just thinking about them.

"Congressman," she suppressed an eye roll, "I have heard that before. Anyone making that claim is glossing over the fact that hundreds, if not thousands of reputable scientists have looked at my work, quoted my refereed publications in their own work, and none have said it wouldn't solve the problem we all face, whether we admit to ourselves that we face a problem or not. Everyone agrees these things will be costly, and there is never universal agreement in science, but there is a large majority consensus that, in all likelihood, this is the most cost effective way to solve the problem we all face."

She stood there with her mind racing. She wasn't sure if she just shot herself in the foot, perhaps destroyed her career before it got started, or if she had just done herself a giant favor. Her heart was racing and she was hoping she didn't start to sweat from the nerves that were now jumping up and down all over her body. She knew that the solutions she was pushing would work, she also knew this man could crush her hopes and dreams.

"You are just like your mother. Smart, quick, and beautiful. I am sure you aren't aware of this, but I met her a number of times, and people who never met her really missed something special. She was one of the smartest individuals I ever had the pleasure of knowing. I was saddened by her passing. You have my sincere condolences. To lose your mother at such a young age, in such a public way had to have forced you to grow up quickly. I think they played that video on the news every night for a week, then it made its way around social media for months. Then, of course, there were people that claimed the whole thing to be a hoax, the whole thing was just tragic. I meant no offense, but remember that if we end up working together you will have to face people in the U.S. Senate and sometimes they can be…well, assholes," he said.

She blushed quickly not expecting that, "Thank you Congressman Fox, I was unaware you had met either of my parents. People who knew both of them say I take after my father more than my mother, but I appreciate the compliment."

"I used to vacation at their hotel. You were too young to remember. But they introduced me to you once. You couldn't have been more than eight or nine. You seemed very precocious, even then, and you have certainly not lost that trait.

"You look nervous, but don't worry. I am officially on your side. I will need to have you explain far more of the details of this whole thing to me. I don't want to go to bat for you without being ready. Please, sit," he said pulling out a chair and offering it to her.

"Can I send someone to bring you a drink?" he asked.

She finally noticed that he was surrounded by his staff, and various other onlookers who had been watching the exchange. She had been so focused on him that the fact that they had gathered an audience had escaped her. Thanks to her appearances at so many public events, she had become accustomed to people staring at her and barely noticed now.

"Some ice water, and perhaps a glass of Syrah?" she asked.

"I was watching your work discussed on a news station, I don't remember which one, you weren't on at the time, and they referred to something called artificial sunspots. What are those, they didn't really explain it, and are they a necessary part of your solution or just some media buzz word?" he asked.

"They are very necessary but I don't like that name very much. Sunspots are a natural phenomenon, and we could never make them happen artificially. Even if we could, they are short-lived, and, even though they are dimmer than the remainder of the surface of the sun, they are still too bright to do what we need. I understand the analogy that gives rise to the term, although it is not strictly accurate." She could feel the wine taking effect and reminded herself to drink more water.

"However, there is a pretty easy way to think about what we want to do. We are going to build giant sunshades, or sunglasses if you prefer, that will serve to block some of the rays coming from the sun. We can build them with dynamic controls so that we can change how much light they let through over time if the need arises. For instance, right now in 2038 a certain amount of light should be blocked to get our temperature back to a lower level, and thereby get our climate to reach an average equilibrium from an earlier year but, perhaps in 2050, it will be either a greater or a lesser amount of light intensity that is desirable, depending on human behavior and natural cycles that are known to cause climatological shifts.

"Don't worry, the sunshades don't need to be the size of the planet. That is a very common misconception. They would be placed at an equal gravity point between the Earth and the Sun that works greatly to our advantage. We can deploy them robotically, so we don't even need to send very many astronauts that far out into space. This point in space will allow us to reduce the total cost dramatically. Enough design work has been done on that sunshade material itself so that this is something we could start mass-producing relatively quickly. We do have to develop and demonstrate a number of new technologies, but nothing that hasn't at least seen a laboratory demonstration, so we have high confidence that they will work at this larger scale. In other words, this is not nearly as risky as the early Apollo space missions that resulted in a man walking on the surface of the moon.

"Now politically speaking, if you will allow me to intrude on your area of expertise, this would be a huge job producer. There would be tens of thousands of jobs created in the short term, and thousands would remain in the long term. That is before we consider any ancillary support job creation and the economic multiplier those jobs exert on the service oriented portions of the economy. Our employees would hire nannies, dry cleaners, and interior decorators, and buy homes and groceries as well as everything else we expect in modern society. In short it would be a nice economic boost," she said stopping for a sip of wine.

"Now you are speaking my language Doctor," he said with a sly grin. "There is one thing I have never understood in all the times I have seen this little passion project of yours discussed. How are we going to get so many huge structures into space at the correct location? It sounds like the equivalent of many cities of high rise buildings must be built then launched."

"There was a NASA Institute for Advanced Concepts report that was written way back in 2006 that provides an easier way. There is a technology that blows bubbles that would shade a portion of the sun. In other words, we send uninflated bubbles into space. The liquid that becomes the sunshade material after inflation will be 100 million times smaller in volume when launched than the deployed size of the bubbles. We actually have since developed a way of deploying flat structures rather than spherical bubbles, so that they can be titled to control the amount of sunlight that is blocked," she said, reminding herself again to drink more water than wine. This wasn't a night to get drunk and she had a very low tolerance for alcohol. She could feel it starting to make her brain go fuzzy and this wasn't the time to be thrown off balance, and alcohol could do that.

"We are still talking about many thousands of launches. That is going to be costly. Last I heard every time we send up a rocket it is many millions of dollars just to reach low earth orbit. To get that far out where you want to place the sunshades, I am assuming that the cost goes up dramatically. That is unless you have a solution for that as well," he said, looking hopeful.

"Well Mr. Fox, you are in luck. All we have to do is stand on the shoulders of the scientists from the last century. There was a man working in the 1990s by the name of Derek Tidman. He was a physicist who came up with the concept for a delightful device that very few took seriously until well after its initial field demonstration. It was called a Slingatron. It is a hypervelocity gyromechanical sling. Here, let me show you the principle," she said picking up a bowl and an olive she plucked from an aide's martini, not noticing the surprise on that aide's face.

"If I place this olive in the bowl, and gyrate the bowl in a small one-inch circle, then you will see that the round olive synchronizes in circulating around the larger bowl circumference at the same rate as I gyrate the bowl in the small circle. The bowl is about five times larger in diameter than the gyration circle. Now the olive is travelling at about five times the speed at which I am moving the bowl. If I tip the bowl, then the olive will leave at that higher speed." She tipped the bowl and the olive flew about a dozen feet away from the table. She had demonstrated this before and could control the direction in which she shot the olive so that it did not hit a guest, but it did roll some distance away on the floor. She secretly enjoyed the surprise this demonstration generally created in her audience. She once hurled an olive at a wall so hard it was squashed upon impact. Something that she hoped to be able to duplicate every time, but so far had only achieved once.

"Now imagine a higher technology, much larger version with a speed multiplication approaching one hundred, and you will have an idea of how we can reach escape velocity at a very low cost per launch. In fact, the more launches we make, the lower the marginal cost per launch."

"Well, the obvious question is, how many launches are needed, and what is the total cost? But I'll save that for another day. I am willing to wager that you know the answer to my next question, what is the estimated cost of global climate change are right now on a yearly basis?" he asked.

"In 2030 globally it exceeded five trillion US dollars," she said quoting the U.N. estimate.

"Well, Doctor, it looks like you and my staff are going to become close friends. We are going to have to prepare you for testimony but, for the moment, you have done good work. Now, before we part company, because I have many other people that I need, not necessarily want, to speak with tonight, I have someone I would like you to meet. You are single correct?" he said with a smile.

Here we go she thought. She thought for one night

she would be free of this, especially from him, but apparently that was not to be. But she needed political support from this man, so she would be polite to whoever it was.

"Yes Mr. Fox, I am," she said with a smile she hoped didn't look too forced.

"Well, there is this Chemist over here, ahh yes. Dr. Franklin! Here is the woman I wanted to introduce you to. Scott Franklin, meet Emma Hallbar. Both of you have shown up at many of these events without a date for so long that you both have to be very tired of being 'setup' by people. Exchange numbers and start attending together just to keep the setup artists at bay will you please? You will then find these events so much less annoying," he said.

She wasn't sure what to say, she was embarrassed at her first reaction. She took Dr. Franklin's hand, shook it and blushed.

"I appreciate your time Congressman," she said shaking his hand, after which he turned and walked away.

"Dr. Hallbar, I have seen you on television. I asked him not to set me up or try to do something like this, especially with you, so if you like we can just speak politely and sneak out separately later," he said.

"The Congressman actually has a reasonable idea. I don't know about you, but I get very annoyed at meeting the 'perfect person' every few days. If I may ask, what is your field of Chemistry?" she asked making small talk.

"Atmospheric Chemistry," he said. "Your work needs no introduction. I heard what you were saying to him, and am familiar with your passion-driven quest. I'm on your side by the way."

"Wait, you are that Dr. Franklin? The one who has been searching for ways to do large-scale chemistry in the upper atmosphere to pull out pollutants and make them into something useful, or at least something we can harvest neatly so that it isn't a problem down the road? I assumed you would be much older," she said hoping she hadn't gone too far.

"Well, like you, I knew early on what I wanted to do and pushed hard for it. I thought maybe we could fix the environment doing upper atmospheric chemistry, but I can't come up with a model that doesn't turn into really nasty rain someplace," he said.

"I know. I have read your papers and I think you are onto something. In time you may get there. I'm not sure we have time, but I like the approach you are pursuing. Honestly, I never do this but I would love to have dinner and talk. Maybe together we can brainstorm some ways to have my work and yours combine in a useful way. Long term I really think I can get the temperature under control. Once we get that done we will still have some cleanup to do, and that is where your work would come in handy, provided I can give you a stable environment in which to work," she said.

"I would enjoy that, and stability would really help," he said.

She wrote down her number, said her goodbyes and made her way home. She hoped that in the long term this night would lead to the end of the professional road she had been traveling. She certainly felt like she had taken a major step forward.

Chapter Seven

Emma woke up every morning to the aroma of fine coffee wafting through her apartment. She had been a chronic workaholic since before her parents died, and it only increased while she was in college. During prep school she never had any problems, but now coffee was the only way she could get going in a reasonable amount of time. The coffee maker had an auto timer which would start brewing thirty minutes before she woke up. The aroma helped her get out of bed instead of repeatedly hitting the snooze button.

This particular morning she was sticking to her routine of email over coffee and was surprised to see that she had a dozen or so emails from Congressman Fox's staff. He was keeping true to his word to provide some help with the preparation of the testimony for the Committee on the Environment.

Her apartment was set up for a person who was married to their work. The living room doubled as an office, which surprised the few guests who had seen the place, but she preferred it this way. Most home offices found in apartments were, to put it mildly, cramped. This arrangement gave her space for a large working area and lots of room for bookshelves to hold a wide array of reference material and multiple video monitors. She had several different computers in the room, each with their own 3-D full immersion displays, which made displaying data to spot trends much easier.

One constant in the every room, including the

bathroom, was a television that was almost never turned off while she was awake. They were always tuned to a weather station so she could monitor for surprise major storm events. She wanted to know about them as quickly as possible. The place was designed for functionality, not social functions. Those were for elsewhere.

She had even filled the dining room non-traditionally with a treadmill instead of the typical table and chairs.

She didn't eat at home often, but when she did it was at the breakfast bar that separated the kitchen from the living room. Many of those meals consisted of yogurt or some form of takeout. The most commonly used appliance in the kitchen was the coffee maker. The only other item that came close was the microwave, but the coffee maker was far and away the winner.

She was going through the emails from the Congressman's staff and found there were some good but fairly basic questions. She had no trouble convincing them that there would be no challenges posed in the form of the technical aspects that she couldn't handle.

She thought the questions about which contractors or companies around the country could build the larger, more expensive components were irrelevant and bizarre. That was a problem for another day and it didn't really matter to her so long as the thing got built. She brushed them off as nothing and focused on the questions she couldn't answer as easily.

She was always tripped up by the politically oriented questions. She was learning from the staff how to deflect those in a way that wouldn't offend the person asking the question in some way she didn't anticipate. She didn't understand why these mattered, as she was a scientist. She even posed that question back to the staffers pushing the politics. They made it clear that if these weren't handled exactly right the entire hearing could quickly lose focus. This frustrated and annoyed her, but she played the game, pushing feelings aside and trying to remain focused on the bigger goal.

Her day was quickly consumed by this preparation.

After a full day of emails, phone calls, and a video chat or two, the staff decided to recommend to the Congressman a slightly different path. Prior to her testifying in front of Congress, she should meet with a special committee at the National Academy of Science, perhaps including committee members from the National Academy of Engineering. The Congressman had the ability to get such a group organized in short order. This group would be full of world-renowned experts whose letters of recommendation would be beyond reproach. If she could get some of the well-known members of these organizations on her side, then congress could not possibly throw a scientific roadblock in her way. The only problems left would be political, and the committee hearing could turn into a formality.

She found this to be a brilliant idea. She recommended adding to that group some representatives from the National Science

Foundation. Then no one group could say that they had hand-picked their panel members to get a consensus with ease, and no major American scientific organization would feel slighted.

Somewhere in the middle of all of this work, she received a text message from Dr. Scott Franklin. She was surprised to find that she was not annoyed by the distraction. He wanted to take her up on the offer of dinner and discussion. She had instantly said absolutely, she would be happy to meet him anytime he was free. He sent her a message back within minutes saying he was available tonight, and 7:30 might be a good time if that worked for her. She agreed without thinking, excited about the prospect.

A staffer on a conference call said that because it was running a bit late, he wanted to call his wife and tell her he wouldn't be home in time for dinner, and to go ahead and eat without him. That caused Emma to look at a clock to see what time it was.

Oh Crap! 6:15 already? Where had the time gone?

"Wow, I had not realized how long we have been at this. Why don't we call it a day?" she told the group on the phone.

There was a chorus of "agrees."

She still had to get ready to go. There was work to do if she was going to be "dinner ready" in appearance in time to meet him.

She turned off her computer without looking at another word. The small apartment became a flurry of showering, hair, makeup, clothes, no not those pants, the other ones. Where are they? There they are, with the dry cleaning she had just picked up the day before.

She was out the door almost exactly one hour after the whirlwind began. It had to be a record. Luckily Scott had picked a restaurant that was a very quick cab ride from her apartment. The robotic cab drivers linked to traffic computers were getting much better at finding the optimal path through traffic to any destination. In a city with as many people as Washington DC, this was a huge time saver.

She barely made it in time, at 7:29 to be exact. She would have preferred to be earlier, but at least she was on time. Late would never do.

She walked in, unsure where to meet him, glanced around and spotted him in the bar sipping something before the hostess had a chance to say hello and ask what size table she needed.

She waved her intention to meet him to the hostess and walked toward the bar. As Emma approached, she could not figure out what he was drinking. After a lifetime in hotels, normally she could tell at a distance.

"Hi, sorry I kept you waiting," she said.

"Oh, that's ok. I have not been here that long and it is very nice to be out of the house for the night, without being at some formal event. I don't know about you but I tend to work most nights. Being single does that," he said breaking the ice.

She couldn't help but notice that he was a bit

awkward in his dealings with people one-on-one, to the point where his sentences came out with pauses in all the wrong places, at least when he isn't talking about technical subject matter. She knew him by reputation and was certain that if he was talking about either atmospheric chemistry or pollution mitigation, that awkwardness would go away.

"What are you drinking?" she asked.

"A Mai Tai. I never know what to order at a bar and I picked up the taste for them at a conference in Hawaii, but I could never get used to the fruit so I get them without things floating around," he said.

Now she knew why should couldn't tell what it was. The fruit was missing.

He continued, "They are different from most cocktails, without the harsh alcohol kick of drinks like a Martini. They do a really good approximation of the Hawaiian version here, so whenever I come to this place I have one," he said rambling a bit but starting to appear less tense. She wasn't sure if she made him comfortable or if it was the rum in his drink, but either way she thought that something about him was different.

She looked over at the bartender, "I'll have one of those, but I like the fruit," she pointed to the glass and smiling at him when she asked for the fruit.

"Have you ever been to Hawaii?" he asked.

"When I was younger we used to do layovers there when coming to the United States mainland. Later, airlines started servicing our island with longer-range flights and we didn't have to stop there any longer. But I can't say I ever spent a vacation there. Given where I am from, it just didn't make any sense," she said with a smile.

"Oh, I just assumed you were from the States. Your English is perfect, and without accent. Where are you from?" he asked.

She couldn't believe he didn't know. This story had been on the news for so long it was refreshing to find someone who didn't instantly start asking questions about her mother, or what it was like to be from such an exotic place, that to her was just home, "I grew up in Tahiti, for the most part, but I live here now."

"Oh, I'm sorry. I didn't know. I know the Island was pretty badly damaged by one of the cyclones. What was the name of that one?" he asked.

"Cladis," she said. She was really taken aback that he didn't know who her mother was. It was nice in so many ways to have someone talking to her, for the sake of talking to her.

"I guess I understand your passion for your work a little better now. They say that was one of the first of the big storms caused by climate change. But it certainly has not been the last. The Island has been hit hard many times now, and from what I understand it is almost uninhabited," he started to say something else but took a sip of his drink instead.

Her drink arrived, "Well, that was long enough ago that I have made my peace with it. Tahiti used to be an Island Paradise, but now it just serves as a weather station for scientific instruments and, really, as a target for massive storm systems. I haven't been back since just after that first storm. I hear that it is very overgrown now and hard to even get ashore. Very few non-military pilots will even chance it, and then only with helicopters. The runways are all destroyed, and the dirt runways they tried to fashion seem to get washed out pretty fast. It is almost purely accessed by boat these days, so you have to really want to go there."

"I can't say that I know exactly how that feels, but I sympathize with your feelings," he said.

"I really like being here in the continental U.S. better anyway. Living on an island is different than people think. They are great places to vacation, but living there gets more than a little boring after a while. Think about it, after you have lived there for a short while, then you will know everyone, and have seen everything more than once. If you want to go more than an hour drive from home, then you have to go to an airport and fly someplace. So it gets a little, annoying isn't exactly the right word, but somewhere between annoying and boring," she explained.

"Wow, I never thought about what it would be like to live in a place like that. But I guess that would be about right. You know, every time I see you on television I think you look really familiar. Now that you mention Tahiti you bear a striking resemblance to a Tahitian actress, I can't remember her name," he said obviously struggling to recall the information.

"You mean Adena Eliana Hallbar. She was my mother. My parents were killed in Super Storm

Cladis," she said. She didn't really have a hard time talking about it anymore. She was surprised that he didn't know that. It seemed like it came up so often on the news that she just took for granted that everyone on the planet knew it. It was refreshing to find someone who didn't know everything about her personal life. She couldn't help but think that he had to be just as dedicated to his work as she was to hers. Perhaps he was the kind of man she wanted to get to know better. She had shut off that part of her life for so long it seemed strange to consider it, but here she was considering it.

"Oh...I am so sorry," he said. Unlike most people who told her that, he seemed to really mean it.

"Now that you told me her name, I know I saw her in a movie or two, and of course all those ads for Tahitian tourism where they had her say her name and Tahiti as often as possible in 30 seconds. I should have put two and two together from your last name I suppose. You know, to be honest with you, when I watch movies it is often hard to tell that there is an actor behind the character. But, in her case she always seemed to be more than just a beautiful woman. I can see now that I have met you that if genetics works the way I think it does, then she had to be a very intelligent woman. You certainly inherited her looks, and your intelligence must have come from your parents as well," he said.

"Thank you, I appreciate it. I made my peace with the whole thing years ago. I do what I do because it is the right thing to do, but their death did push me to go in this direction. I was originally going to go to medical school, but this became my calling.

"Many people lost family, and I am no different from the rest. My mother's career has given me a degree of access that I might not have had otherwise. That has helped me to bring public focus on this problem. I hope that they would be proud of my work if they were still alive," she said reaching for her Mai Tai, and thought it was a very good one. "This really is a good drink. Some are too heavy on the rum, others too heavy on juice, but this one gets the balance right. Whoever programs their drink mixers has done it perfectly."

"Not to change the subject too abruptly," Scott said, "but I spent my day reading as much of your work as I could. Not the fluffy news stuff, but the actual journal articles. Do you really think you can control how much light passes through these sunshades with enough precision to keep the results reasonable? I mean, too much cooling would also cause issues just as bad as the warming has caused. Getting outside of the 'Goldilocks range' would cause more problems than it solves," he asked.

"We absolutely can stay within the 'just right' range. It has been demonstrated in the laboratory as well as on a very large scale. So, to answer your question specifically, yes, I am certain we can achieve the desired results with enough control to not go too far. Even if we did go too far, we can quickly adjust the sunlight reaching the Earth as needed. That is one of the really nice things about the design, the dynamic control capability. We can fine-tune it in the future as atmospheric conditions change. We can even turn it off if we want," she said.

"By large scale what do you mean? To be big enough you can't just build a one square yard size device. This thing is going to have to be very large in space. Large scale can mean so many things to so many people, as we both know. Sometimes the engineering is where the whole thing falls apart. Scientifically something looks like it will work but in practice it fails," he said.

She had been in political discussion mode all day. She had forgotten to reset her brain to talk to a scientist, and a well-trained one at that. "I'm sorry, I have spent my day answering questions for politicians on the same topic. I didn't mean to try to throw you a generic answer to a specific question. If you will permit me to put my scientist hat back on, we have demonstrated multiple sunshades in low Earth orbit that were one hundred meters in diameter. We showed that we can easily do even larger ones at the Lagrange point, but it is not necessary to make them larger. We will be launching a very large number of them, and it's the total area that matters. The largest problem we have to overcome is station keeping. Once constructed these things will reflect sunlight and become, essentially, solar sails. We will have to keep the structures in the right place, but we know how to do that."

"I can imagine that would be a problem but not a scientific one. That sounds like pure engineering. Something we can solve.

"When you say 'control the light that passes through,' do you mean just light intensity across all wavelengths, or can you block out only certain rays leaving others?" he asked.

She was impressed with the question. Most people wouldn't think that deeply about it. He was obviously a thinking, as well as attractive man. Maybe the Congressman had set her up on a real date without realizing it. However, she had no doubt, had he called it that she would have refused.

"The current design reflects sunlight from the UV to the infrared in a reasonably uniform fashion, although if there was a reason to, we could design the reflective coating to be wavelength selective. If you have a motivation to be spectrally selective, we could do that, although it would increase the cost," she said wondering why more men weren't like this. Most just wanted to stare at her, and rarely her face, for reasons only they could fully understand. Many men would say anything they had to in order to sleep with her, like she was some kind of rare score card. One scientist checked off on the "list."

"That's interesting. How long do you think it will take to get to the desired global average temperature? I found a paper that was based on some of your work that claimed it would be in a single season. It was written by a physicist and that seems like a bizarre claim even for someone in your discipline," he said with a smile. Good-natured scientific rivalries were common between physicists and chemists so she didn't mind. She was glad to be considered one of the crowd. She even had some chemistry jokes of her own if she found an opening.

"Well it is just a matter of reaching thermal

equilibrium. We know the sunshades will give us the desired change in temperature. They should work analogously to sunglasses, and how long the globe takes to react is a function of how we use them," she said. "If the paper you refer to is the one I think it is, they assumed that in the short term we would shade more than needed for long term equilibrium in order to speed convergence on the desired average temperature. It is possible to do that because we will actively control the amount of shading, so that we can react to measured changes. However, it is costly, and perhaps wastefully so, to build a much larger shade than needed to reduce the temperature to the 2020 average level that is my recommended goal. It is also possible to get into an unstable temperature oscillation if we overshoot. So my design converges to the 2020 level over a period of three years, but falls below the 2030 temperature average in less than one year."

"Ok, I can see the wisdom in that. In the upper atmosphere we have jet streams and winds that are engines of equilibrium, just as ocean currents are down at the surface. My only concern is that there may be some violent shifts in weather as the cooling starts to take effect," he said.

"Well, that is a risk. But think about the trade space. Storms that are shockingly violent occur now. These things never happened before; at least not with the intensity we see them today. So, if the variations increase before they decrease to the 2020 level, isn't that the right thing to do? Isn't it also a strong possibility that they will continue to get worse if we do nothing?" she asked excitedly.

"Well, if you are correct, this is very exciting. I believe you can stop heating on a global level. Everything else is just a question of engineering it properly," he raised his glass. "To the solution we all deserve." She picked her glass up and clinked it against his.

"To what I hope will be the first of many dinners," she said, looking forward to an evening with a man for the first time in years. Hopefully she could get him to talk about something other than work.

There had been nothing in her life but work for so long that she was starting to realize just how much she missed having a social life that didn't involve a work function.

She had long since lost sight of her work-life balance skills that she had developed in prep school. Perhaps she could at least discuss the arts with someone this interesting. Perhaps there could be a future for her other than textbooks and computer systems; at least she hoped there could be for the first time in years.

Chapter Eight

Emma was lost in thought about how her life had changed. When she was a university student, and had first learned what the National Academies of Science and Engineering were, she instantly revered them and she hoped one day she would be invited to become a member.

Now, as she sat down to defend her ideas in front of a special panel they were convening at the request of the United States Congress, she couldn't help but think that this was just the opening act of something much larger. She never thought she would get to the point in her career where the National Academies were an opening act. That she was sitting here, ready to be questioned by this esteemed panel, and not at all nervous made her realize just how far she had come in life.

In the briefing room she sat at a table with two chairs and a variety of computer interfaces, so that data or designs could be pulled up on a moment's notice. Her table was positioned a few feet in front of a larger set of tables with ten chairs. Each of the ten seating positions had a nameplate. She instantly recognized all of those names as world leaders in a variety of subjects directly applicable to the proposed climate solution.

The panel members filed in and sat behind their nameplates. While she knew who everyone on that panel was by their professional reputation, she had never seen many of them. In some cases she had pictured someone much different. For instance one of the male scientists was surprisingly small of stature, yet a titan of the physics community. This was the panel to find a flaw in her plan, if one existed. She was confident they would not. Perhaps that made her arrogant, but she had been working on this diligently for years, and her work had already withstood much scientific scrutiny. She knew if she could keep her mind straight, this would go smoothly.

She had her fifth date with Scott later in the day.

Wow, five, already. She had been hoping to build a friendship so that they could attend various Washington social functions together, as the Congressman suggested, and avoid the madness that was the line of "perfect matches" people insisted on thrusting upon them. Perhaps it was because they weren't set up as a match that events had taken this course, but they were already in what was her most serious relationship…well, ever.

The chairman of the panel came in, took his seat and the room became quiet. The man in question, Professor Roberts, had a Nobel Prize in Physics and was known to be a very harsh but fair critic. If you had not thought out the details well enough to fully convince him of your assertions, then he would be critical. But, if you were completely prepared, and your work was also accurate, he would be supportive. He was widely known to be hard but fair.

He was the perfect person to lead this meeting. He had a solid reputation, was well respected, and his credentials of achievement were impeccable. He wasn't just an ivory tower theoretician, he had built things…big complex things.

"Good morning everyone. Doctor Hallbar, thank you for taking the time to come and speak with our panel," he said.

"Good morning Professor, thank you for the chance to appear here today," she said.

"By way of introduction for our internet and television audience, we have convened this combined National Academies of Science and Engineering as well as the National Science Foundation Panel to review your extraordinary claim that you can control the climate of the entire planet Earth. Perhaps direct control of the climate is not precisely your claim, but you do say that you can help us stabilize the average temperature at the very least," he said. He appeared to be trying to correct a common misconception before getting things went too far.

He paused a moment before continuing, "As we understand it, one of the reasons that your solution to climate change is interesting is because it is agnostic about the source of that change. In other words, it does not matter whether the global warming is due to the actions of humankind or is simply a natural variation, your plan claims to solve the bizarre weather shifts we are experiencing. We have all reviewed your proposals, papers, and various clips from some of the media appearances you have made. We believe that the idea can work if properly constructed, that isn't in question, provided some other minor questions can be answered. We will get to those questions in good time. However I, for one, have real questions about your projected costs. No project of this size has ever been attempted. Can you help me understand how you think your cost projections are accurate? Often for programs of this scope, the initial cost estimates turn out to be drastically understated."

She was ready for this, "Yes sir I can. You are probably concerned about the question I get often. How can the cost of what I am proposing be so much lower than other proposed solutions? Have I overlooked something they have not?

"In the case of the solution we are discussing today, the largest cost isn't the solar shades, or even the control system, those costs are minor in comparison. Rather, the largest cost driver for anything we want to do is the launch.

"Since the dawn of the space age, we have been sending man and satellites into space using rockets. Looking beyond rockets there have been some, at least politically, untenable approaches using nuclear or fusion explosive propulsion, electromagnetic rail guns, and several other concepts to achieve orbital launch that experienced some combination of technology and public acceptance issues, or inefficiencies that raised their cost. I have extensively published peer reviewed cost comparisons for those that are politically tenable, and capable of performing the thousands of launches solar shading will require within a short period of time. You have been provided with copies of those publications in advance of this meeting. I have also made comparisons with all published climate repair approaches that do not require space launches. Those cost comparisons also favor the program I have proposed, when you factor in the fact that my design provides nearly real-time control of the amount of shading. The scale of the problem we need to solve requires us to go big. It will, unfortunately, be costly. But the sunshades are the least risky approach out there.

"For our solution, it is possible to get into orbit using a gyro-mechanical payload accelerator called a slingatron. It is far less costly than the alternatives, and there is no need to rebuild a launch rocket every time we send something up, or depend upon other costly rebuilds, such as those needed for rail gun erosion. In addition to the reduced capital and maintenance costs, the energy input to kinetic energy output efficiency can be orders of magnitude higher than using a multi stage rocket. The energy input can use electric motors, and we can generate the electric power with dedicated on-site modular nuclear reactor power plants. This architecture could, in principle, drop the cost of the launch by more than a full factor of *1,000* per unit of mass compared to rocket launches. My conservative cost estimates assumes only a cost reduction of 100 times with a large reserve to cover any unforeseen contingencies. Now as far as other cost drivers," she stopped as one of the panel members cleared his throat and indicated with a hand motion that there was a question to be asked.

"Doctor Hallbar, good morning. I am professor

Grigo. With regard to this mechanical launch, I have not heard of this before. Can you go into some detail please?"

"Certainly. We use what is known as a slingatron. With this type of device, our launch payload would be accelerated along a rigid track. It works by small gyrations, not rotations, of a larger diameter track. An ordinary example of gyrating something can be seen in the way some bartenders mix drinks. They put the drink in the glass and move the glass stem in circles. This, in effect, mixes the drink.

"The continuous centripetal force experienced by the payload in a slingatron will act as the accelerating force. The force is continuous as the payload passes through the machine because of the continuous gyration.

"I brought with me a small model of a simple slingatron. This particular one has a circular tube about twenty inches in diameter that is supported in such a way that it can be gyrated in about a two-inch diameter circle by a small electric motor. The velocity at the edge of the small circle is about one foot per second. When I place this small steel sphere in the tube, it synchronizes with the electric motor, so that it makes one circle around the twenty-inch diameter tube every time the electric motor completes a rotation of the two-inch diameter circle. This gives us a ten to one velocity multiplication. If I set up a simple target that consists of a piece of cloth hanging from this small support, and then release the sphere by opening a hole in the tube like this, then you see that the sphere just impacted the cloth at precisely ten feet per second due to synchronization with the drive motor.

"We would use a large spiral track of an optimized design that is shown in the reference material I have supplied. The optimized design has a much larger multiplication of the electric motor drive velocity than our simple circular demonstration tube can provide," she concluded.

"The most obvious question to me," started a person on the panel she had not met, but knew by her reputation as a very intense skeptic of the work of anyone not directly affiliated with her personal lab, "is why you won't have the same problems with wear that a rail gun has? Those devices quickly need replacement rails, at velocities well below escape velocity from the Earth."

"Professor Rapteur," Emma began, "the rail gun erodes its rails where the electrical current flows between the rail and the payload. We do not have an electrical connection, and in fact our payload rides on a gas bearing and does not touch the tube at all. We place an ablative coating on the payload, and as it accelerates above a kilometer per second, the ablation creates the gas bearing whose friction actually decreases with velocity. This was demonstrated in the 1990's. I believe that when you have taken the opportunity to fully read all of the publications I have provided, that you will be satisfied that the slingatron does not suffer from this problem, which was proven by demonstration, and it is the best overall choice, and by a very large margin."

"When you say electrical power, it sounds like we

will need a lot of energy. How much energy, and what are these small modular reactors you mentioned," professor Grigo asked.

"The reactors are a product that was proposed as a concept in the 20th century, and has been commercially available from several different power companies since 2030. They functionally resemble the nuclear reactors that are used in naval vessels such as aircraft carriers and submarines.

"I have performed a trade study that examined the cost per year of implementing my approach compared to the cost saved by mitigating the climate change damage caused by flooding and storms. As you can see in that study, the optimal strategy is a rapid construction of a significant number of slingatrons, each of which are launching multiple payloads per hour, twenty four hours a day until we have an initial shading capability to block up to three percent of the sunlight the Earth would otherwise receive. Earlier studies had shown the need to block about two percent, but the rate of increase in greenhouse gas emission we have seen was not correctly anticipated in those estimates.

"Once the initial capability is in place, the majority of the slingatrons will be cannibalized for maintenance parts, to support the ongoing launches that will be needed to maintain the orbital system. This may sound wasteful, but the trade study clearly favors rapid deployment, because the cost of climate change for our economy is growing rapidly and is expected to exceed ten trillion dollars annually in the next decade. Rapid deployment can save orders of magnitude more than the cost required to do so."

"Thank you Doctor Hallbar. You appear to have some compelling ideas and have done your homework. I was unfamiliar with these modular nuclear power devices. How long would it take to construct these reactors, and at what cost assuming no special permits are required or red tape needs to be cut?" Professor Grigo resumed.

"The devices are currently constructed on an assembly line for sale around the globe. They can be delivered in six months after the order is placed, compared to the many years typically required for one of the massive nuclear reactors that are still being built in many parts of the world today. They can be shipped partially assembled instead of constructed on site. The final assembly and nuclear fuel is added after delivery," she explained.

Dr. Roberts asked, "I know that sometimes cost estimates contain large uncertainties. What have you done to reduce risk and uncertainty in those estimates? No one has ever built a slingatron for orbital launches on this scale or for an orbit this high."

"We performed several risk reduction demonstrations." She took a sip of water before continuing. "We built a high velocity prototype. Then we scaled the demonstration to the largest size we could afford.

"That prototype slingatron showed us that we can do this. We reached a velocity of 8 kilometers per second with a ten-gram projectile. It is not a useful payload size, but we did demonstrate an orbital velocity. Just as predicted, the friction continued to decrease with velocity and in fact was unmeasureably low at speeds above 6 kilometers per second. The data is provided for you, and everything met or exceeded expectations. Please note that the slingatron launch for the sunshades is to low earth orbit. After the sunshade structure is deployed in space, UV cured, and sprayed with an opaque coating, it will be inserted into the higher Lagrange orbit with low acceleration electric thrusters."

Dr. Roberts said, "I have to agree with you, in that this is the cheapest way to get us to the Lagrange points. That is the right place to put your device, and I think your overall design will work. All of that assumes this is a problem that we need to solve. That is for other people to decide. Would anyone else have suggestions or questions?"

"Yes, I would," said Professor Cash from the University of Texas.

"Certainly Professor," she said.

"You seem to have dotted many i's and crossed many t's but I have to ask one thing. This system is capable of dynamic control. You say we can control the system as our global temperature goes up and down over many years in response to differences in greenhouse gas emission, for example. What is to stop someone from taking over the system and holding the planet hostage with continued heating or insane cooling?" she asked.

"There have been leaps in cyber security and we will

implement extreme physical security. Our system will not be controlled from the typical planetary World Wide Web. Our communication system will use free-space point-to-point links, and would not be connected to any network outside the control room itself. The Command Center will be securely located under Mount Imperium. Immunity from electronic warfare usurping the control sequence is assured by our unbreakable quantum cryptographic encoding. Physical occupation of the control center is the only way someone could usurp command of the system. If a weapon of mass annihilation destroys the control center, the system can operate for a year autonomously with graceful loss of capability, although its effectiveness will, of course, continue to degrade over time if no maintenance is performed. There is enough time to create a new control center in that extreme case. If we do elect in the future to reduce the number of shades, those we allow will, within a few months, move away from the Lagrange point due to the pressure of sunlight upon these very low density objects. They would no longer shade the earth. There is no long-term issue with uncontrolled shades. This is also the primary reason that we need continuing maintenance and refueling of the station-keeping thrusters."

"Thank you. I now see that you have even considered security in your planning," she said.

Dr. Roberts sat up straight, "Well ladies and gentlemen, do we have any other questions?" there was a silence in the room. "Well, may I call you Emma?"

"Absolutely," she said feeling that she now had them.

"Emma, you appear to have addressed the few questions we were left with after reading your proposals. We will help you prepare for the Congressional hearing and certainly provide letters of support. Now, may we take you to lunch and we can chat a bit more on some of these finer details?" he asked.

"Sure, if I can make a phone call and bring one more person along, an upper atmospheric chemist who is familiar with the project," she couldn't stop smiling.

Chapter Nine

"You have to learn the rules of the game. And then you have to play the game better than anyone else." – Albert Einstein

Emma, like many people, had a regular breakfast routine. She would keep the television, typically the weather station, on in the background, check her email, and eat yogurt with a side of coffee. This was a no yogurt but extra coffee kind of a morning.

The panel meeting went so well that she and Scott had gone out to celebrate instead of just grabbing the quick meal that was typical for them, considering their hectic professional schedules.

Scott had joined the group for lunch and they had both spent the afternoon with some titans of the scientific and engineering worlds. It was a day to remember. Afterwards she wanted to go celebrate the giant leap forward the project had made. If she was still living on Tahiti, that might have meant some kind of beach activity with a huge fire, some friends, possibly a roast pig and a few drinks, but here in Washington that really wasn't an option. They tended to frown on open fires in the local urban environment. She really did miss the beach and warm weather.

She usually tried to avoid thoughts of home as they caused her to become depressed. Today was different. Today there was a chance to move forward to a climate fix that could make Tahiti back into the paradise it once was.

Near DuPont Circle the city started to taper off a bit, and the pace slowed down ever so slightly. There was also a restaurant she had heard about and always wanted to try. It was a fondue place and apparently, according to her friend, the perfect place for a date.

Shocked that they had a human cab driver instead of a robot, they gave her a reasonable tip and went inside. The place was very unassuming. Normally DC restaurants had people running this way and that shouting things to each other. Patrons were often loud, bumping into one another, looking at smartphones and wondering how fast their entrees would arrive.

They were greeted by a very soft spoken host who asked for their name, turned to the assistant next to him, whispered the table number to her, and off they went. On the way to their table she marveled at the ingenious layout. Each table was a sort of booth with very high walls between them for privacy. The seated guests could talk to each other and enjoy an intimate meal, without having to listen to the table next to them. Many of the tables were designed specifically for two people, allowing them to sit side-by-side instead of across from each other. The menu wasn't the nicest in Washington, but it was unique, and the place certainly had the best atmosphere she could imagine for a young couple wanting to take their time during a meal.

This was her first real adult relationship, and she

wanted this kind of intimacy. It wasn't just physical, but emotional connections that she missed. She felt that connection with him, and was hoping tonight they could delve deeper into that side of their relationship.

In the past she had dated a few guys, and had a boyfriend or two. She had even slept with two of them, but this was different. She was getting to know Scott in ways she had never gotten to know anyone; especially not a man, and she now believed that they were building a future together while she was trying to save the planet so that there would be a future.

One of her former graduate school classmates kept asking how many dates they had been on. She had kept track for a while, but now decided it didn't matter anymore. She could remember virtually every moment they had spent together but had long since given up trying to remember how many lunch, dinner, or museum dates they had enjoyed. She often found her mind drifting to some of her favorite moments while she was working. That type of distraction had never happened to her before. Work had been her focus ever since she stepped out of the prep-school dorm. She wondered once, after their first date, if she should find a way to get out of this and refocus on her work, but something about him made her not want to do that.

He wasn't a distraction. She admonished herself for even thinking of that word and him in the same sentence. He made her feel good and challenged her to be better all at the same time.

She was learning much from him about how her

work could impact the upper atmospheric chemistry that provided the Earth's ozone layer. Some of his input had gone into a few new calculations that would change some aspects of the way the sunshades were operated. Their construction would remain the same, but day-to-day operations would be much better with input from someone like him.

Dinner had run a little late. It had been a spontaneous event, and therefore not well planned. He had an early meeting, so their cab dropped him off at home before bringing her back to Georgetown. It was a shame, she was hoping to invite him back to her place for the night, but there would definitely be a next time, or first time depending on how she thought about it.

They had made plans to meet for dinner tonight. She said she would plan it out from start to finish. The only other thing on her schedule for the day was to re-read her notes in preparation for her Congressional hearing.

After the last few days of intense preparation she knew she was ready, but she went over the potential political questions again. She had spent the better part of a decade in preparation for the scientific portion what she was about to face. What she needed today was to clear her head and relax emotionally. Stress could cause her to make a political misstep, and she couldn't afford to do that.

She realized that if she had invited Scott in for a drink last night there would have been a problem. It had been so long since she kept wine in the place that she could not have offered him anything but coffee or water. Then she looked through her closet and decided it was time to find something new to wear for dinner. It was a girly thought, and that wasn't typically her style, but she wanted to wear something new for him. Everything she owned was either work clothes, or very comfortable clothes that she would only wear at home when no one was around.

All of this meant that she was going to go shopping today. Luckily everything she wanted to purchase was available near her apartment right in Georgetown. In fact, everything she needed was within walking distance so that she wouldn't have to try to find a place to park.

There were some fantastic looking boutiques right around the corner that she passed every day, but had never visited. Surely there she could find some clothing that wasn't designed for work. She didn't mind wearing work clothes to go out, but they were all very conservative.

Tonight was one of those rare nights when she wanted to show off that she was a very attractive woman. Many people told her over the years that she had her mother's movie star good looks. She was never comfortable with that fact, but thought that for once she could just go with it and see what happened. She wanted to move their relationship forward, and his personality wasn't one to do that too quickly. She didn't want to scare him, but she also wanted to make her desires more apparent, now that she had admitted to herself what they were. Something about Scott's personality was such that she might have to hit him over the head with a hammer to get him to make a move. Tonight she wanted him to do that.

She left her apartment and made her way a few blocks over to one of the stores that she had passed many times but had never entered. It caught her attention because they always had such beautiful things on display. Some part of her always wanted to go in there, but she hated spending too much money on herself. She rarely spent any of the inheritance that her parents had left to her. She had always lived on her own income, and really below her means, with the exception of her car. Perhaps it was time to indulge just a little more than she typically did.

As she walked into the shop the sales woman met her almost immediately.

"Hi, can I help you?" she asked.

"Yes, I wanted to find something special for a dinner date that I have tonight. I always see this place but never seem to have time to come in. I want something that is a bit more colorful than my normal work clothes. Maybe something more like I would find back home, I'm originally from Tahiti, but not so bright and flashy, just a hint of that," she said.

"You *are* her. I have seen you on television, Doctor Hallbar, right?" she asked.

"Guilty as charged," she said.

The sales woman proceeded to help her by showing her a number of dresses. She settled on one that had some deep green patterns that complemented her skin tone without being too over the top.

The sales woman was nice enough, but asked too many questions about her "famous mother," the tragic deaths of her parents, and many other things that she had answered a hundred times, and most of it had been on television often. She had long ago realized that she wasn't just going to be a scientist, but a public figure, and this was the price one paid for that decision. The woman asked if there was a special occasion, and for whatever reason, Emma had gushed with information about Scott.

She felt like she was back in prep school and talking about a prom date. Perhaps she was being a little silly, but it didn't really bother her that much. Perhaps it was because since before her parents had been killed she had mostly ignored this part of her life. Emotional attachment was not something she had allowed herself in recent years. She decided it didn't matter that she was acting like a schoolgirl. She had a date, and she was looking forward to it. Then, she would move on to meet with Congress, get the project funded, and perhaps see the solution to climate change through to the end.

Now that she had taken care of the clothing part of her day, she went shopping for food and wine. She had a small wine fridge back at her apartment that had been the home for a single bottle of absolutely horrible wine someone had given her over a year ago. She thought it could hold thirty bottles, so she had some space to fill. She bought fifteen bottles of various reds and ten whites. Luckily this store would deliver by drone later in the day, since she couldn't carry it all with her. Then it was on to the grocery store.

She wanted to start slow in her quest to cook more often, so she wanted to just pick up a few things. She bought a pineapple, a few mangos, some fish and a few spices that reminded her of home. Some of the chefs that had worked in her father's hotel had taught her how to cook from time to time, and she felt confident she remembered the lessons.

After the grocery store, she made her way home just in time to meet the wine delivery and get ready for dinner. They planned to drive to the restaurant this time instead of taking a cab, and he was going to come pick her up at 7:00.

She was watching the window, waiting for him to arrive. When he pulled up in front of the building she was so excited she rushed out to meet him. He drove a sedan that was a few years old, something typical of younger scientists. It was nice without being too flashy or too expensive, but she didn't care about anything other than his company.

She climbed in his car and hugged him, "Thanks for picking me up. I have looked forward to this all day."

"You look fantastic. I think this is the first time I have seen you out of work clothes," he blushed a little at his statement. He was obviously checking her out, which had been her goal.

"Actually, I bought this specifically for tonight. I never thought my project would get this far this fast, and I really never thought I would meet such an interesting man along the way," she said hoping she wasn't coming on too strong. She was pleased that he had checked her out and that he seemed to have to keep reminding himself not to stare at her breasts.

"I know today is special for you and this is a celebration, but I hope you don't mind that I just pulled this out of the closet," he said obviously feeling a little guilty for not putting much effort into his appearance.

"It is different for men. At least that is what my mother used to tell me. I am far from the most fashion forward person. Your gender's fashion doesn't change every day. It has been, more or less, the same for decades. But I wanted something that was a little closer to home. I normally try not to look like my mother, which is a challenge, but today I don't mind," she hoped she wasn't laying it on too thick.

"Well, I am glad you wanted to do it for our date," he said. As he pulled out of the parking lot, he reached over to hold her hand as the cars automated driving system took over.

"Scott, I also want you to know that I get the fact that I picked a very expensive restaurant. My parents left me a large sum of money so rather than beating up a scientist's savings account, this one is on me," she said.

"Well, I suppose I will let you do that, and not allow my manhood to be insulted. I also hope you don't mind if I stare just a little bit?" he said attempting to flirt and not being very good at it. He was cute anyway, she didn't mind.

"Not at all," she said coyly.

She didn't live all that far from the French Bistro they were going to for dinner. They pulled up outside, and they saw a variety of what appeared to be news crews on the restaurant side of the street, and a huge gaggle of people on the other side of the street, with a few police vehicles in between. She wondered what had happened to attract the attention. Perhaps it was some kind of accident with the news there to cover it, and the people were just there to look?

"Oh, I hope everything is ok. That is our place," she said as they pulled into the valet.

As soon as she stepped out of the car the camera crews from two news agencies and one television entertainment news crew ran towards her, "Doctor Hallbar! Can we ask you a few questions," one of them said.

She didn't bother to answer, but they all started shouting more; now she was embarrassed by the dress.

When she stepped around the side of the car the crowd that had gathered got sight of her. They erupted all at once. She finally saw that they were holding signs and were obviously not fans of her work. They all seemed to want to slash government spending and seemed to think that what she wanted to do was a waste of taxpayer dollars.

One of the reporters could be heard above the noise.

"How does it feel to be one of the most famous scientists in the world and to have the idea that could stop the weather from destroying more cities, and killing more people? What do you want to say to those people who think your ideas are just a waste of money and that the entire situation is just hyped out of proportion by scientists trying to enrich their own careers at the expense of the taxpayer?" One of the legitimate news organizations asked.

"How does the daughter of a famous actress become what could be the world's savior according to some, and economic destroyer by others?" The entertainment reporter asked trying to drag her mother into things.

"I have no comment at this time," she said, just as she heard her mother say so many times. She had not expected this. Had she been in the right mindset she might have been able to come up with a sound bite for them to use but today her mind was elsewhere.

She knew what would happen if they went in the restaurant. They would wait outside through dinner and be there when they came out. Reporting the entire time about her clothes, Scott's clothes, the car, they would conjecture about their relationship trying to determine if they were coworkers or if it was romantic. They would do anything they could to fill airtime. It was at times like this that she thought that there were just too many stations, and there was too much airtime to fill.

One of the protestors was throwing things their direction but their aim was not all that good. The police quickly went to the guilty party and handled the matter.

"Scott, let's just go," she whispered in his ear.

"Ok," he waved the valet off since the car had not

been moved yet.

They got back in the car and drove away.

"I am sorry about that. It happens to me from time to time, but never to that level. Usually it is at a conference when I give a keynote. I have no idea how they found out where I would be. It looks like they have been here a while. Let's just go back to my place, I can cook for you," she said.

"I have never experienced a paparazzi or protestor attack before. It isn't as much fun as people think," he said.

"No, it really isn't," she offered.

"Well, at least my brother will finally believe I am dating the famous Doctor Hallbar, daughter of an Oscar winning actress, once he sees the news," he said.

"He didn't believe you before?" she never thought of herself as someone that special.

"Actually he did, but my mother on the other hand doesn't buy that I am dating anyone. She thinks I am too obsessed with my work," he said.

"Perhaps I can meet them someday," she said hoping she wasn't assuming too much, or perhaps scaring him.

"Well, they don't live too far away. I am sure we can arrange that."

"Excellent, and hopefully you will enjoy my cooking," she said nervous that the quality of her cooking may have declined during the intervening years without practice.

Chapter Ten

Emma was exhausted. She tried everything but she couldn't sleep all night. It wasn't just that she felt closer to Scott than ever. It was more than the fact that she had enjoyed watching him sleep for some reason. It had been their first night together, and she was certain it would not be their last.

She was tired, but excited, or was it nervous. Sitting here waiting to give testimony to Congress meant that her project was about to take a giant leap forward or be smashed into pieces.

Congressman Fox had warned her that her testimony today, while an important step, might not lead directly to funding. There would probably be more work to do after today. However, he said, if it all went well, things would be downhill from here.

News cameras were all over the room. Normally that might make her nervous, but she was getting used to it. She didn't understand why so many people found her interesting, but for some reason cameras seemed to follow her everywhere.

She was ready for today, Scott was amazing, and things, according to Congressman Fox, should go relatively smoothly for a Congressional committee meeting. She was cautiously optimistic, because he would be in the room, and in charge of the meeting.

He had personally called her while she and Scott were eating breakfast this morning to let her know that he had spoken to every member of the committee and believed he had them all in line. That gave her a confidence boost going into this morning. His call clearly showed that he was managing every aspect of the day, and hoped to make it as successful as possible. He was bringing to bear the full force of his own political power.

This meeting, and the television audience it would draw, caused her to dress in her most conservative business suit. She had carefully applied her makeup, not too much and not too little. She didn't want to seem like she was seeking the spotlight, merely that it managed to find her. Long ago she had evolved from seeking the spotlight for her message, to not being able to avoid it.

Scott was sitting in the gallery watching, and she wasn't sure if that made her feel better or more nervous. She didn't care about the television cameras, but she wanted him to respect her, and he would know instantly if she made a mistake. She did not want anything to happen that could work against their relationship.

She couldn't worry about him, she needed to focus. Congress always arranged the room for these testimony sessions the same way. She was seated at a smallish table with three not very comfortable chairs behind it, a microphone in front of her along with her nameplate, and a few video screens surrounding her should the need arise to show some data or drawings. The Congress people sat on a risen floor that was a bit higher than hers, and it was behind a nice solid piece of what appeared to be mahogany furniture designed specifically to make them look larger than they were. The members all had overstuffed, very comfortable looking chairs, nicer microphones, and nameplates with the names etched in wood. The overall effect of this was to make the people on that side of the table appear above anyone merely testifying. People sometimes referred to politicians at this level as "masters of the universe," which was a curious and inaccurate phrase, but one that was meant to mock their inappropriate attitude of superiority.

Congressman Fox told her to ignore much of the trappings, and that it had been done this way for a very long time as an intimidation tactic designed to get people to tell the truth faster. It seemed more humorous than intimidating to her, but she could see how it might impact people who were not prepared or had something to hide.

She had been seated for fifteen minutes, waiting since five minutes prior to the designated starting time. She expected the meeting to begin at least thirty minutes after the scheduled time, but that would not prevent her from being early. She needed to continually convince herself that the congress people were not in some "smoke-filled" back room meeting that would destroy the chance that today would end well. Intellectually she knew that wasn't the case, but that didn't stop the panic from appearing in her mind every minute or two. She had prepared, but all of the years of school, papers, conferences, and sleepless nights could now be derailed by a simple bad answer to a political, non-scientific question.

She mindlessly flipped through her papers

wondering what the "gotcha" question of the day would be. She was reasonably sure of two things. There would be at least one such question, and that this would be a long day.

Several of the Junior Congress people were already present in the room and were looking at their watches off and on, wondering how much more time the senior members would take. Protocol said that all members would be seated before the Chair, which was Congressman Fox. The senior members knew how to watch for him, the younger ones had yet to master the art. He had sent her an email to expect him twenty to thirty minutes late so that he could do some last minute; "wrangling" was the word he had used, of the other members. As she read the email, she could hear him say it in his southern accent. So that meant that any moment now they should be getting started.

She was taking a sip of water when she saw Congressman Fox standing in the hall talking to someone. Senior members were scrambling to quickly be seated before he walked in. She wasn't certain, but he appeared to be in a good mood, smiling and occasionally laughing, speaking to someone she did not recognize.

As he came in, he went directly to his seat at the center of the table. He got things underway without looking around to ensure attendance of the other members, "Ladies and Gentlemen, take your seats. I would like to get started. This meeting of the House Committee on the Environment has now come to order. We have with us today Doctor Emma Hallbar.

She has gone through considerable effort, as well as personal expense, to bring to the attention of the world that there is a way to heal the planet from the issues caused by what is often referred to as human-influenced climate change, although she merely refers to it as climate change, and has publicly said many times she could care less about the cause, only the cure. Doctor Hallbar, good morning. Thank you for joining us. Before we get started is there anything you would like to say," he said throwing her a pre-arranged opening to make some statements that would chase some politics out of the discussion.

"Thank you for having me here Congressman. I would like to just reiterate one thing. The solution we have proposed and the work done to date is independent of the source of the global climate change. We know that the average temperature of the Earth depends upon the amount of energy it receives from the Sun. Controlling the sunlight incident upon the Earth is agnostic with respect to the cause of Global Warming. This solution will allow control of the average temperature of, and therefore the energy available to, the Earth's climate without regard to whom or what caused it to change.

"We are all aware that these changes have caused very strange storm systems that are much larger, and harder to predict, than ever before. They form in new ways, and are unpredictable in their behavior. As long as we all agree that these climatic changes are happening due to unprecedented heating, then we can fix that problem, and someone else can worry about blame. I, for one, just want to see the problem solved," she said.

Someone from the Congressman's staff had explained to her that each end of the political spectrum had their own "evil" to which they assigned blame for these climate shifts. She hoped that her statement would alleviate much of the political yelling that was likely to be aimed in her direction soon if she didn't throw out some way to provide "cover" to both political parties.

"Thank you for clearing that up. So often here, at these meetings, we get caught up in determining who is to blame for the problems facing us and we lose sight of what is best for the future. I appreciate your resolve and desire to fix this problem rather than just rant and rave about where we should assign blame," he said smoothly.

He took a deep breath before continuing, "I would also like to add to the official record something with which all of the members have been made fully aware. You have recently met with a special panel of the National Academies of Science and Engineering, and with some folks from the National Science Foundation thrown in for good measure. The panel was chaired by the Nobel Prize winning scientist, Professor Roberts. They dug into your proposal at length. I have had my staff distribute copies of some glowing letters from this group stating that what you propose to do, if implemented properly, can do what you say it can. They leave it up to us to determine if it is worth the cost, but they say that among all of the proposals they have seen, this is the lowest cost viable option," he said leaving the other members of the committee very little wiggle room for questioning the science or engineering aspects of the sunshades.

"I also want to get into the record that every member of that panel you met with has said you are impeccably credentialed, and that you have thought through every essential detail of your proposal. You have assembled the right scientific team, and you are ready to go to get these sunshades put in place and functional. They say that you may have the attention of the world in ways no scientist has in a hundred years, but that doesn't make you any less qualified or prepared, in spite of media assertions to the contrary," he said.

As he spoke, she noticed that some members of the other political parties were shifting uneasily in their seats. She found it interesting and educational to watch a political master at work weaving his way through what could have been very rough waters in her testimony. It could have been her imagination as to why they some elected officials were shifting around uncomfortably, but none of the members of Congressman Fox's party did anything but sit back comfortably and listen.

"One thing that has come under much criticism, and not undeservedly so, is the overall cost of what you propose. This thing isn't cheap, it may be the lowest cost way to do this, but the bottom line price is still substantial. Some will say yes, but what is the cost of doing nothing, and I will get that. But I know I speak for every member here when I say how can we justify this expense?" he asked.

His staff had prepared her for this.

"Congressman, I agree that these costs are high. The question, to me, isn't merely the cost of doing nothing as measured in dollars, it is the human cost. We all watch the nightly news and see these super storms pop up with no notice and no predictability. It happens so often now that we have just become accustomed to it, and they are now considered normal. They are often deadly, yet not the lead story anymore, because they have become so common. It is down to just a scorecard and the numbers are abstract. 200 people here, 1,200 people there. These things may have become commonplace, but there is nothing normal here. This isn't something we have to put up with. We can engineer our way out of all of the death and destruction, if we have the will to do so.

"The most recent of these was a cluster of tornadoes larger than the world has ever seen in recorded history. Let me be specific. The cluster had a larger number of tornadoes and each of those making up the cluster were larger than any single tornado on record before Superstorm Cladis. It broke every record imaginable for this type of storm. Record after record after record-breaking storm has occurred. Tens of thousands, if not hundreds of thousands of people have been killed; families have been exterminated. Entire regions, such as Tahiti, have been rendered essentially uninhabitable.

"Some have said that because I was born in Tahiti, before becoming a US citizen, that this is just a personal quest. They are right; this *is* personal. It is personal because I, like everyone here, am a human being, and I would like to survive until my body decides I have lived long enough, not until some storm ends my life early. This isn't just about dollars and cents. This is about lives, human lives. We can argue over the costs of this versus the costs of that, but how many more mothers, fathers, sons, daughters, how many future Nobel Prize winners, or artists must we lose before we act is the question that should be asked of those people saying this isn't a problem worth solving.

"There will not be a short road to a solution. Science has shown us how to fix what has been destroyed, but we must also build for the future. This thing I have pounded the sand saying we should build isn't my solution; it belongs to everyone. We have stood on the shoulders of giants who have come before us and merely managed to find a way to put together pieces designed for other purposes to fix this issue," she said hoping she hadn't gone too far, sounded too preachy or even alarmist.

"Thank you Doctor. I have no further questions and I will turn you over to the ranking member of one of the Minority Parties, Congresswoman Mitchell. Congresswoman," he said as he pushed a button hidden from Emma's view on the panel in front of him.

"Thank you Congressman Fox. Doctor Hallbar, I want to thank you for joining us today. The members of the minority party and I have spoken before this meeting today and we think we can save us all a lot of time if I speak for all members. Is that ok with you?" she asked kindly.

Emma wasn't sure if that was true, if she was actually kind, or if there was something political going on, but there was only one correct answer,

"Absolutely Congresswoman, I am here to help in any way I can. However you would like to proceed is fine with me."

"Great. We have all reviewed the documents you submitted. We are uniformly appreciative of you putting everything into layperson terminology. That must have been challenging given the complexity of the subject matter. I agree with you that the cause of what is wrong with our planet is irrelevant. Like you, I just want to fix the problem and move on. What we should focus on, as you have pointed out, is that solution. That is refreshing for someone entering these halls and I thank you for that," The Congresswoman said.

"It seemed the most logical thing to do, Congresswoman," Emma said, unclear about where this was going. She started to grow a bit nervous, as it was the unknown question that bothered her more than anything and she smelled a trap coming.

"We have but one question. You say this is a worldwide problem. You have done some impressive work on your own without government funding at proving that these sunshades will work. That is unique among people coming to these budget meetings, and it has not gone unnoticed.

"Our one question is this. You say that this is a global problem, involving every human on the planet. Yet you ask the United States and the United States alone to bear the costs of this. Why should we? Is there another way to pay for this? How in the name of the taxpayers I represent could we possibly sit back and say that this is a reasonable approach to building your proposed solution? Doesn't that seem a little bit bizarre of you to assume the good will of the American people to that level?"

Emma was upset with herself for not anticipating that question. She should have seen it coming. She knew there was always one question that could not be predicted, and this was a good one.

She didn't panic, she merely took a deep breath and remembered all of the times her father had an upset guest in the hotel, and turned the problem back on them when seeking a solution to something that had made the guest unhappy. Normally the guest would settle for a free dinner in the restaurant. She was pretty sure that wouldn't work in this case. She looked at Congressman Fox hoping for some help, but he was looking down at his table scribbling something on a notepad.

"Congresswoman you are correct. The way I have proposed it will have the United States pay the costs. As a scientist I don't really have the skillset needed to get the nations of the world to come together to do something like this. I have spoken to scientists all over the world who have a desire to work on this solution. I can say that the cooperation within the scientific community is worldwide in nature. If there is a way to get the nations of the world to cooperate on funding of the sunshades, then I would be happy to work to make that a reality," She hoped that she had threaded that needle and didn't make the Congresswoman angry.

She looked over at Congressman Fox who was smiling just slightly. Perhaps she was imagining it, but then again, maybe it was real. She was certain she had come close to what he would have said.

"Doctor, I appreciate that, and rarely does anyone tell us they don't have the skillset for anything. Normally people here are so eager to please they will try anything we suggest. It is admirable that you know what you can do and what your own limitations are. That is how I know you will help make this project a success."

Emma's heart skipped a beat. Could that really be true? Could this be the only question before some positive step forward is taken? It couldn't be that easy.

"I would like to make a suggestion. I would like to get Congressman Fox to ask the President to request a special meeting at the United Nations in order to make an appeal to the nations of the world to pay for this project in some kind of equitable cost sharing methodology to be identified later. I see the scientific utility, I can see the need, and the cost in certainly the most reasonable I have ever seen for a solution to the climate change problem. Congressman Fox?" the Congresswoman said.

Oh great she thought. They just punted the decision to someone else. The people here chose not to decide anything themselves when they could ask someone else to do it for them. She grew frustrated and hoped her discomfort did not show, especially on camera. Anger was not the emotion she hoped to feel at the end of the day.

Congressman Fox reached over to turn on his own

microphone, "I think that is a fine course of action." He turned in his seat to look at Emma, "Doctor Hallbar, I think I speak for all members of this committee in saying that you have done some outstanding work. No one here is going to stand in the way of funding these sunshades, and we hope the nations of the world follow the United States in this desire."

A message suddenly appeared inside her smart glasses. Someone on the Congressman's staff wanted her to know that even if the United Nations said no that the United States would do it anyway. She breathed a sigh of relief and hoped that was true.

The Congressman continued, "I will call the President as soon as we are done here to ask for his support. As there appear to be no more questions I think we can dismiss this meeting for the day. Doctor, thank you for your time."

She sat in disbelief. She assumed this would be a brutal day, not a twenty-minute discussion. Could this really be happening? Was this really going to be funded? She looked around to see Scott smiling ear-to-ear. The television cameras all shut off as she gathered her things.

Something had happened behind the scenes that she was blissfully unaware of. She only hoped that it wasn't something that would throw roadblocks up later.

***

Emma could not believe her eyes. She was watching on the monitor from outside the General Assembly Hall in the United Nations Headquarters in New York City. The members were inside voting on a motion to jointly fund the sunshades. So far support was overwhelming, at least inside the building.

Outside there were protestors from all over the world. They held signs, shouted things, and from time-to-time threw whatever they had with them at the police and National Guard who were keeping them back from the UN headquarters. The police had set up barricades, but they were light and wooden, making them largely useless. There were enough protestors that they could be heard even this deep in the building.

She was with Scott and The President of the United States, Malcom Wilson. She would have never guessed that she would meet, much less spend time watching this vote, with the President. But there he was.

Scott, for his part, was taking everything very well.

The entire world was going to rally behind this solution and put their trust in her to make it work.

"Emma, it looks like you are going to get your funding," said the President.

"Yes, Mr. President. Now it looks like the politics is over and the real work can begin," she said.

"Oh, Doctor Hallbar, if you think the politics of this is over, then you really are new. I would be remiss if

I said I didn't have lots of reservations of putting you in charge from here on out. I think you are the person to run certain aspects of this project, but we need to have someone on your side who can help manage a program of this size. Not scientific problems, not engineering questions, but administrative and political ones," he said.

"I'm afraid I don't follow. They said we have funding; what else is there," she said feeling confused and a bit unintelligent for not seeing what was obviously coming next. She didn't care if she was in charge or not, but she had always just assumed she would be. Titles didn't matter to her. It was the completion of the project that was the important part.

"Doctor, whenever this much money runs around there will be arguments over everything from who supplies the screws to exactly where you build the thing," said the President.

"I see…." It hit her that he was right; this would be really hard from here. There were going to be contractors fighting for every piece of supply work they could get. She had just assumed that all decisions could be made scientifically but as soon as he said it she knew she was wrong.

"You need a good, solid, program manager for this. You run the science, they run the overall program. I will find someone for you," he said as someone came and whispered something in his ear.

"Ok, you and your boyfriend here need to come with me. There is apparently a massive storm popping up just off the North Carolina coast that will soon impact the entire East Coast. It is forming just offshore and will move westward. I need to get back to Washington, and I suspect that your flight is already cancelled. You are officially invited to fly back with me on Air Force One."

She was grateful for the offer, even though she rolled her eyes a little at yet another sudden storm. They had to get this project built and operational quickly; there was no time for politics. There had been enough of that, however she was sure this was just the start.

Chapter Eleven

Andy Smith sat patiently waiting to see Congressman Fox. He always found the offices of Congress people interesting. They were always impressive compared to the offices of people paid at a similar level in the private sector. Being the CEO of a combined aerospace, defense and energy company, he was running one of the largest corporations on the planet. People three levels down from him in the corporation were more highly paid than the Congressman. Yet he was now waiting, happily, some 40 minutes past the pre-arranged starting time of their meeting.

There was a commotion in the hallway, and then Congressman Fox appeared in the office. He was surrounded by his staff, each of whom had a different agenda item requiring his "immediate" attention. He waved his hand and they scattered. Andy walked into the inner office behind the Congressman, "Thanks for waiting Andy. I do apologize for the delay. I don't have to tell you that Washington DC does not have a time efficient culture.

"I wanted to let you know that both the President and I appreciate the efforts of your lobbying group to influence the right committee members so that we could carry the day with all parties before the Congressional hearings on the Sunshade Project got started. The only way this thing is going to happen is with multi-partisan support for what will turn out to be the most expensive space program in the history of the world. I think we actually have enough support that the outcome at the United Nations is now irrelevant."

"My group will do whatever we can, Congressman. This program has greatly reduced the pressure we are seeing to curtail fossil fuel use. As you know we have been working to wean ourselves from non-renewable energy sources, but burning fossil fuel energy is still a major source of the economic health of the nation, and will remain so for at least another decade," Andy replied.

Andy reached into his suit jacket pocket to hand the Congressman a stack of large checks, large enough to startle him, "The main purpose of my visit is to make a major contribution to your political re-election campaign fund. Similar contributions are being made to the President's fund, and another to the party itself. I understand the protocol, and I will give the checks to the appropriate people, but I wanted you to see them first."

"My gratitude extends beyond words, Andy," the Congressman sat down hard behind his desk. "If we can make the way we sustain both the economy and the climate to converge, that would be a truly wonderful thing for the future of the world, and I think this nation should lead the way."

"Well said Mr. Congressman. I trust that you will

appoint the correct management team for this project, which is especially important for one of this monumental scale."

"Yes, the President is taking care of that. Dr. Hallbar is a competent scientist and the 'mother' of this system concept, as well as very popular worldwide, however we will appoint a proven program manager over her to guarantee this goes off the way we want it to."

***

Andy watched the buildings go by from the back of the taxi on the way to the office of his senior lobbyist. The lobbyist was known around town by his nickname "Straight." He was a Native American and insisted that his given name was actually, "Straight Arrow Truth Teller," but no one believed it. In spite of that, the man did enjoy an amazing level of positive influence with members of every major, and a few minor, political parties.

Andy walked through the reception area and directly into the office, "Straight, we have several priorities to cover. For the record, for the next several years the Sunshade project is absolutely your job number one. That will not change unless we have moved much further from our current dependence on fossil fuels. That won't happen soon, so do not get distracted from this goal."

"I of course understand completely Mr. Smith," Straight began, "although I think we may be underemphasizing some other agenda items. I have a list."

"Give it to me, Straight," as Andy never tired of saying.

***

As the door closed and Andy departed on his way, Straight took out his cell phone and dialed his father. He spoke in his tribal language, as he always did when he wanted to be sure no listening device or snooper would understand anything said.

"Father, the project is moving forward. They are going to forever alter nature," he said.

"Son, thank you, we will start to make arrangements," Straight's father replied.

"Thank you, I wish the tribe success," he said as he disconnected the line.

***

Once Andy landed in Dallas, he did not go home, he went directly to his Corporate Headquarters. He walked from his limousine to the Executive Conference Room. There he found, either in person or attending via 3-D conference, all of his Division Vice Presidents and his Vice President for Business Development.

"Ladies and Gentlemen, the Sunshade project will be moving forward. This will secure us billions of dollars in business expansion, rather than the drastic contraction which would have resulted from a restriction, if not an outright ban, on fossil fuels. That ban will now become irrelevant, as there is an alternative solution to global warming.

"Now that our existing business planning will not be interrupted, we need to add a new top priority to that plan. That priority is to win the largest share of the contracts for the design, construction, and operation of the Sunshade Program. We have the opportunity to double our federal contract business within a very short period of time. The Vice President for Business Development will be the focal point for collecting the Division plans. I want to see a preliminary plan by the end of the week. I hope to be pleasantly surprised with the bottom line growth projections. This is a time of unprecedented opportunity for all of us!"

Chapter Twelve

After so many rapid changes in her life; testifying before congress, votes at the United Nations, meeting the President, and getting a ride on Air Force One, Emma knew it was time to admit to Scott, out loud, that she was madly in love with him. She had argued with herself for a week about how true that was, but she decided that it was true, and he deserved to know. It was a strange thing for her. It was the first time she had ever said it to someone that wasn't a blood relative. Life had been a series of firsts in the past few months, so what was one more.

It happened on Air Force One as they were racing back to Washington. They were running away from yet another potentially deadly storm. Something about the emotion of the day made her spontaneously say it. As a scientist she usually had a plan for everything, but for this it was merely an instinctual response. Scott had immediately reciprocated. That excited her far more than she had expected, but she also felt relieved, as there was no plan for what to do if he wasn't in the same place. He actually admitted that he almost said it a few times but was reluctant, because he didn't want to scare her. They shared a laugh, which helped with the stress of the day.

They immediately decided that it was time for her to meet his family, starting with his parents. The only family she had left was an Uncle who lived in Hawaii. Even growing up she barely knew him, so meeting her family wasn't necessarily going to be part of the near future. She had kept up with some of her mom's friends out in California, and even thought of some of them as family, but that could also wait. His family, however, had been excited for some time to meet the famous Doctor Hallbar. His mother had asked every time he spoke to her, and finally he could get her off his back.

His family was not that large. He had just his parents, a brother, one aunt and an uncle who could wait. His parents and brother lived close to each other, slightly north of the Chesapeake Bay, just a few hours drive from Washington DC.

They decided to take her car for the visit, since it was more comfortable. She encouraged him to drive. He was reluctant because he didn't want to damage it, but she insisted. It was just a car after all. She didn't care if he accidently put a dent or ding in it. In any case, with the current combination of sensors and computers, if you engaged the automated systems, then the "driver" could put the seat back and take a nap while the car drove itself to a pre-programmed destination. Even in the more passive mode the car would stop the human driver from making many common mistakes that would result in an accident. When these systems were first introduced, it had taken years for full public acceptance and trust of self-driving cars, but every car at least had driver assist packages now. This car was just more automated than most. She really liked the style of hers. All of the gadgets were merely a perk. His was a little older and didn't have much of the automation, but she assured him that he would adapt quickly.

"I have to admit this thing is really nice," he said as they left the Washington Beltway. "I normally don't think about cars all that much. To me as long as I get where I want to go it served its purpose, but if you have to drive, this is the way to do it."

"It is the one indulgence that I allow myself. When I was a kid in Tahiti I used to hang out at the valet counter near the garden at the hotel my father managed. There were always luxury cars arriving and I used to admire them as they came through. Everything from the styling and build quality to the paint finish were things of beauty. When I was older I was allowed to park them. It was one of those things I used to get excited about. One of the very few perks of living in a hotel with a father who ran the place. He used to pick on me for wanting to be a valet, it was how he got his start in the business. He used to say, 'The apple doesn't fall far from the tree.'

"Once I completed my undergraduate work, I bought one of those cars as a kind of celebration, and ever since then I have upgraded every few years. This is just the most recent of those upgrades. I liked it because it isn't too big and it basically drives itself. Plus the automatic parallel parking system really comes in handy around Washington with how small some of those spaces are," she explained.

"Well, you have chosen very well," he sounded distracted as he kept playing with the gadgets.

"Honestly I rarely drive, I usually take cabs or the metro. I probably should take it out more often if I am going to have something this expensive. I suppose I should enjoy it. Now that I am starting to be recognized more often, it might reduce the delays in getting to work if I stay away from public transportation. Then maybe I could be more productive at work, instead of having to come in late because people ask questions or ask for pictures," she said.

"What is this thing anyway?" he asked.

"It is a BMW i6500. It is a little expensive, but my mother made a lot of money in her acting career and my parents never really spent much of it. I guess I am kind of like that, a compulsive saver, but I do like this," she said thinking that what she had just said wasn't totally true. She also liked the designer clothing she wore to work. The interest income on her inheritance was large enough so that she still saved and increased the principal without ever going to work. On top of that, very soon the sunshade program would start pay her, instead of it just being a job of passion. She had been very fortunate to be able to pursue her passion for the sunshades, and work 60 hours per week without the distraction of an employer dictating how she spent her day.

"I really like this car," he said getting used to more acceleration than any car he had ever driven before. If he set the cruise control, then of course the car would smoothly accelerate to a preset cruising speed, but he had turned that feature off. She found it funny that he was playing with the accelerator when most drivers would just engage every automated system possible. She enjoyed doing the same thing almost as much as he appeared to.

"I'm glad you like it," she said thinking that if they ever got married she would have to get one for him as a wedding present. Was thinking about the "m-word" jumping the gun? There was an actress friend of her mom's who was her occasional sounding board for personal issues ever since her parent's passing. She made a mental note to give her a call to ask when it was appropriate in a relationship to be thinking about the potential for marriage. She was the only actress who came to mind who had been married to the same person for almost twenty years. She didn't fault the others for their personal choices. She wasn't here to judge, but she wanted to only be married once. Her parents had been married from the time they were in their early twenties until the end of their lives.

"Whatever you do, don't allow my brother to drive this magnificent vehicle. He has too many speeding tickets already, and he will beg. He loves this kind of thing, and his first act would be to turn off all of the safety gadgets and see what he can get it to do," he laughed.

They passed the time with small talk. His parents retired to live on a few acres of land that they mostly used to keep his mother busy. She tended a much larger than necessary vegetable garden, but she enjoyed giving away tomatoes and peppers to the neighbors. During the winter months she found indoor things to do. Typically some annual craft obsession would take over. Last year it was pottery, but that was last year. This year was promised to nothing...yet.

As they made their way up the long driveway, she saw that the place was really beautifully kept. It was a small cottage style home set back from the main road with a well-manicured lawn. She thought that she might have seen a pond in the distance out back, but it had rained a lot lately, so it might just be an oversized puddle. It didn't matter. The place had a natural beauty. She hadn't allowed herself to think about home much while attending the University, and lately she was starting to miss the inner calm that visits to Tahiti used to bring her. She needed to find another place to escape to on occasion. That universal need for escape even included scientists trying to solve large-scale problems. Perhaps she would find that place here with Scott's parents.

They parked, and as soon as they stepped out of the car, his mother came bounding out the front door toward them with her arms outstretched. His father walked more slowly behind, sporting a huge smile on his clean-shaven face.

"Scott! Finally," his mother said giving him a bear hug.

"Mom, this is Emma. Emma, this is my mother Colleen," he said blushing and trying to escape his mother's embrace.

The older woman was about Emma's height, making her roughly five and half feet tall. She was slender yet sturdy. Emma tried to shake hands with her, but instead was given a hug that almost lifted her off the ground. She looked at Scott who seemed embarrassed, but she found the hug very welcoming, so she gave him a smile, letting him know this was fine, parents do what parents do. She missed this kind of thing. He seemed to be uncomfortable bringing someone to meet his parents, but she found his parents very inviting. She hoped that it meant that she was among one of a very few women to ever earn the privilege of being brought here to meet them.

Scott's father finally made it to the car and rescued Emma from the bear hug, "Will you turn the poor girl loose? Hi, I'm Louis," he said shaking her hand instead of repeating the more aggressive style of his wife. He was clearly several inches over six feet tall and did not appear as if he spent as much time outdoors as his wife. He seemed to Emma to be more like a book reader who would drink coffee, perhaps on the porch, and look at the garden rather than be in it.

It didn't matter. Emma found them both charming.

"Glad to meet you both. Scott has told me so much about you. I feel like I know you already," she said.

"Come in, sit. We have some wine if you would like a glass, or virtually anything else to drink, just name it. Scott, did you steal this car or shall I assume it belongs to her?" his father joked.

"Funny as usual dad," Scott said with an eye roll, handing the key fob back to Emma.

They went inside and made their way through the house to a screened-in porch at the back. The place was decorated just as she had expected. It was quaint, yet comfortable. They even had a baby grand piano that made her want to sit down and play as soon as she saw it.

"So, you are the one we saw on the news hugging the President," his mother said.

"Oh my God, I didn't realize they had caught that on camera," she was embarrassed by that at the time, and now even more than when it happened.

"I have to admit that when Scott first told us you two were dating I thought he had to be messing with me," his mother said.

"No, we really are dating," she said and recounted how they had met, a story his mom did not know, and one she now promised to recount to all of her friends. She swore she would tell everyone that he had to be told it wasn't even for a date, just for a "protector" when he was at other social events, or would have never gotten around to asking her out in anything other than a professional manner. Emma laughed as she had never thought of it that way, but essentially they were supposed to protect one another.

"But I'm not really what you see on television. I am just a scientist, like your son, but in a different field. Some would say that he is actually better at what he does than I am at what I do. His work is, by far, more original than my own. I just represent a very large program that has been proposed in various versions for decades. I found a way to make it cheaper, and I am working to drag it across the finish line. His work on upper atmospheric chemistries is far more cutting edge and has a great deal more scientific potential than mine. It is also much more complicated. I just get more press coverage," she said trying to downplay the fame that she felt had gone much further than she had ever wanted.

"Well, I'm not sure about all that. But I do know that the last time your name came up on the news you were called the potential savior of humanity. Some are saying that you are the next Feynman, whoever that was," Louis said.

Emma started to explain who Feynman was, but decided against it. It wasn't relevant to the discussion, and she hated to dive into a college lecture with her boyfriend's parents.

"The news just needs things to talk about. There are so many stations now that they have to find something to put on them all 24 hours a day 7 days a week," she said.

"Well that is true, but I see you on a whole bunch of them all at the same time. So you are news, honey, as much as you want to deny it. I even saw Scott on the news with you one night. It looked like you two were trying to go to dinner and it didn't exactly work out as planned," Louis said as Scott came back outside with four glasses of red wine on a tray.

"That was actually kind of funny. They jumped us going into a restaurant one night. There were even some protestors across the street who thought I was making all the weather disasters up just to further my career. As if I had the ability to falsify all these events. Anyway, I was in a dress that I had just bought, and I think the sales girl ratted me out on the plans for the night. I heard that one of the shows, lacking anything else to report, analyzed the dress to see if it meant we were a couple or just co-workers. You would think I was a movie star or something. My mother used to get that kind of thing, but me? A scientist? Who cares?" she said laughing with a wave of her hand.

"I saw that segment, and they decided it was a relationship because no one would dress like that for work," his mother said with a wink. "It was a beautiful dress. Scott, I also saw what you were wearing. You can't dress up for a date?" his mother teased him.

"She surprised me on that one actually. Normally we just go straight from work, wearing whatever we had on during the day. It was a very pleasant surprise," he said remembering that night.

She blushed slightly remembering that night as the first time they had slept together. She hoped neither of his parents picked up on that. Louis gave her a look that only a former CIA analyst like him could. He may have picked up on something, but perhaps it was her imagination. She hoped it was her imagination.

"Well dear, you looked amazing. I was a fan of your mother's and I am sure that you hear this often, but you look very much like her. I am sorry for your loss, but I can see what drives you," his mother said.

"I came to terms with it years ago, but I would not be telling the truth if I didn't admit it does drive me.

Her friends have kept in touch over the years, some more than others, but I do what I do because of my parents. When I wanted to quit once or twice, some of her friends pushed me to continue. They are very cause-oriented people who mean well. Most of them have been so nice to me over the years. Some even helped me very early on with some image consulting and advice on how to deal with the press.

"If you really liked my mother's work, some of her friends in Hollywood are going to be doing a tribute to her at a film festival. They even asked me to host, but I not sure I am the right choice. I want to go, certainly, but I think someone in the business should host it. I can get tickets for you, if you don't mind traveling. Some of those things can be hard to get into, and this promises to be a fun-filled, star-studded event," she offered.

"Oh I would love that. We don't get to travel as much as we wanted, but if we have an excuse we would go anywhere," his mother said.

"I'll make some calls, it is in France someplace. I can find out exactly where and someone should be able to tell me the best places to stay. I am sure there are enough people going with private jets that I can even get you a ride with somebody," she said.

His mother was overjoyed.

Scott and his father sat chatting about football as Emma and his mother got to know each other. They chit chatted about various things, but one thing became clear. She may give her son a hard time, but she loved him and was exceptionally proud of him.

His brother wasn't going to make it today; he had been sent on a business trip.

Their dinner plan involved something on the grill. It was summer and his dad enjoyed that sort of thing now that he had fully retired, as long as it wasn't too hot.

They were in the house after eating when Emma's phone started to vibrate. She had chosen some very private settings, and only a very few things would cause it to alert her. She had wanted today to be about one thing only if at all possible.

She looked at her phone and gasped.

"Emma, what is it," Scott asked.

"Turn on the news," she said.

"What channel," he asked.

"If what I see is correct, any news channel, they will all have it," she answered.

He turned on the television and she was right. The first news station had what she was talking about.

The New York news anchor was reading the teleprompter as quickly as possible with still images flipping past in the background.

"As we see, the devastation is widespread. You are looking at downtown London. A storm came out of nowhere. It was clear skies, and then thirty minutes later it wasn't. This is being called the thunderstorm to end all thunderstorms. It is dropping two inches of water an hour on the city, causing widespread flooding," the anchor said.

"They are also reporting winds sustained at more than one hundred twenty five miles per hour. That isn't a misprint?" he asked to someone off screen.

"No…we have that correct, the gusts are up well over two hundred. Lightning strikes all over the city are causing real problems for people trying to leave. They are sparking fires in many of the city's older buildings, causing road blockages as fire crews are being called in as quickly as possible," he said without emotion in his voice. News anchors often did that.

He put his finger to his ear, "We have a new camera coming online. Yes…here you can see Big Ben, the famed clock tower in the background. The famous Ferris Wheel used to be in the foreground. The Ferris Wheel was blown down about thirty minutes ago.

"The flooding is picking people up and washing them out of their homes. Others are being trapped in their homes by the water; it comes in so fast there is not enough time to react; we can only guess what has happened to them.

"We have been told the Royal Family has all but one member accounted for, we will find out who that is and let you know.

"Oh my God," his voice finally cracked.

The screen cut away from the anchor to show just the live video image of London. The famous clock tower twisted in a bizarre way as it fell to the ground. The picture fidelity was good enough that Emma could clearly see three people ejected from the clock tower and thrown into the air. They did not come down within view of the camera, but she was certain what happened. She felt a tear come down her face, quickly followed by a second.

"Big Ben has fallen. We can only imagine how strong the wind had to be for that to happen," the anchor said.

Emma was amazed at how the man could report such disastrous news while showing only slight emotional responses. She thought that he must be one of the people who put ratings above anything else, and this sort of thing would get people to watch.

Scott's father reached over and turned off the television, "Emma, you may downplay how smart you are, but we have faith in you. Please do what you are going to do as fast as you can, before it is too late for all of us."

"My brother went to London for work. He landed about two hours ago," Scott said quietly.

Emma hugged him as hard as she could.

Chapter Thirteen

Any reluctance Emma had concerning the President's decision to put a Program Manager as her superior on the sunshade project was now gone. She had always envisioned herself as the overall project lead, but that had been naive. Financing alone involved agreements between governments all over the world.

A large part of the decision process on a research project in a laboratory is scientific. That was in a lab. This wasn't a lab. In this case almost all decisions were political. She had been horribly mistaken in her assumption that once the money was in place all she would have to do is build the launchers, then get the sunshades into space and functioning.

On paper it all seemed so simple. Unfortunately that is where simplicity left this particular equation.

In short, Emma was happy to have the man the President had chosen occupy the top of the organizational chart and move her over to the box for the lead scientist. The President had named the former Deputy Secretary of State, Cliff Morris. Once she convinced him to stop calling her Doctor Hallbar, at least when they were in private, they had worked well together.

He handled all of the international agreements with an efficiency that seemed to her to be beyond human limits. He had even found creative ways to cope with the never-ending protestors who seemed to be everywhere she went. Now that the program was international in nature, the number of protestors had swollen, now they came from all over the globe.

Everything from the best way to cope with the international protestors to the process of site selection for the slingatrons had turned into a giant political mess. He was a master at navigating those waters, and while she was learning by watching, she wanted no part of solving those seemingly impossible problems. The science was complex enough.

Once it was obvious that there would be a new multi-billion dollar long-term program that would have a central location and satellite locations yet to be selected, the political tug of war began. Everyone wanted the funds associated with a program of this size to reside within their economy. That wasn't the best way to pick a location, and it was a problem she had not anticipated.

Cliff Morris sat down with her one afternoon to brainstorm how to clear away some of these political problems. They decided that telling the truth, and the entire ugly truth, would be the best way to go. All too often when things were starting up, projects would paint a pretty picture. In this case it was easier to go the other way. The pretty picture would be repairing the planet, not the process. The process had aspects that most people would not want to be anywhere near, and if they understood that ugly side, then the politics of site selection may just give way to scientific considerations driving the decisions.

There would be a number of downsides to hosting

any of the launch sites for this project. All that was needed for most nations to lose interest was to list the disadvantages and demonstrate the acoustic impact using a smaller scale slingatron in a laboratory.

There was more to the politics than just site selection. As a result of the amount of money involved, the funding nations wanted to have a way to ensure that no fraud was taking place. A Non-Profit called The World Without End Foundation was formed specifically for the purpose of tracking the money. They would ensure that all participating nations paid what they had agreed, and that the money was spent as proposed. All participating nations agreed to the formation of this organization.

The people running the foundation were an enormous help when it came to dealing with specific political issues. In one case, they agreed to work with Cliff and Emma to do a series of press releases, press conferences and news appearances. The Foundation, on behalf of the participating nations, agreed to impose a condition on any nation chosen to have a launch site within their borders that the site would have to be placed under the permanent sovereign control of the United Nations. Most leaders in the overwhelming number of nations on the planet did not like giving up sovereign control of anything. This made the majority of them reconsider, if not withdraw, their candidacy as a host nation.

A second condition was imposed that reduced the number of interested nations even further. Emma had not been happy about this one. It was decided that site security would be the responsibility of a permanent military presence primarily provided, and funded, by the United States with U.N. oversight. She believed that once things were up and running, the protestors holding signs and shouting at her personal appearances would dissipate. Cliff had told her it was necessary, and once this was put on the program as a requirement, even more nations took a step back from trying to become the host nation.

This military presence was, as explained by Cliff, actually more a necessity than a political convenience. It was clear to him, very early on, that the site would be a target for people far more nefarious than just protestors. Terrorist organizations that would want to attempt to hold the world hostage also had an interest in this project. Holding the facility hostage wasn't the biggest worry. The largest concern was those groups that would want to destroy it. Therefore it was decided that the site would be built as a fortress with defenses against attack from the air, space, ground, or sea.

The final selection of sites was going to depend upon more than mere politics and physical security. Physics, as well as economics, would play a key role. A balance between those two would make the final determination.

The slingatron designs would have to be different depending upon where on the globe each of them was built. If it was placed in a poorly chosen location, the velocity the payloads as they left the slingatron would have to be higher than if the launch site was chosen carefully.

In order to achieve the lowest possible slingatron internal velocity requirements, and therefore make them less expensive to construct, a location near the equator was needed. If located near the equator, the payload would get nearly a one thousand mile-per-hour boost from the rotation of the Earth.

The science team recommended that the site should be as close to the equator of the Earth as possible. The launch angle would be elevated well above horizontal to reduce the amount of time traveling through the atmosphere to a tolerable level for the payload ablative shield. That shield would be required so that the payloads could withstand the heat of traveling through the atmosphere at such a high rate of speed. So the advantage from the earth's rotation would be somewhat less than one thousand miles per hour, but it would still be significant to the overall design.

This decision allowed the team to take the next step in the process of narrowing down the list of potential locations.

Then the team had to consider the environmental factors. These were safety related, as well as the acoustic and ecological issues. The slingatron launched the payloads at supersonic velocities causing sonic booms. That would cause real problems should the launch system be near any heavily populated areas.

Perhaps the most unexpected issue was a group protesting the massive clearing of native vegetation, or the displacement of the local fauna, that would be necessary to build the launch facility. Why that would bring protesters prior to knowing where the facility would be located was beyond most of the project team. What if it would end up in a barren sand desert? Or what if it ended up in some unpopulated, or uninhabitable corner of the world? If that were the case, everyone on the team assumed, the joke would be on them.

Thankfully the job of dealing with this sort of thing fell to the Program Manager, but it was still annoying, until Emma spent time with the chief environmental engineer. He told her that no matter where it was placed, it would require a large effort to write the environmental impact plan. There is no place on Earth where there will be zero impact on the local environment. More importantly perhaps, the effects would propagate around the globe through the migrations and diffusion of living creatures, air currents, and ocean currents. These things really annoyed the project scientists, but she let it go and focused on her part of the project.

But that wasn't the most difficult environmental hurdle to clear; it was merely the most surprising. That gold ribbon honor for the most difficult was reserved for those rare protestors who did some mathematics. There was a way, well known to insurance companies, to calculate actuarial risk with reasonable accuracy. If those calculations were made assuming a very high environmental sensitivity to sonic booms, then the slingatron launches would themselves have a negative impact on the environment. These people argued against the program, and they tended to have some measure of public sentiment on their side.

In the final analysis, the reasoning that carried the day was the same as the argument that convinced governments that this was a good financial investment. The cost of not doing this was orders of magnitude greater than the cost of doing it. The final argument that prevailed was that the environmental disturbance from slingatron launches would be tiny when compared to the certain damage that would be done if climate change was not addressed.

There were other public misconceptions that Emma and her team had to spend time working the news circuit to repair. It seemed to her that some of the media made their living shocking the public as much as they could, even if that meant not telling the entire truth, in the hope that it would increase their viewership. So she spent a lot of time correcting the record. Some reporters misrepresented the slingatron as a giant rotating behemoth that rotated in a circle over a hundred meters in diameter. Initially very few people fully understood how the relatively small gyrations of the machine worked to launch the payloads. She spent more time on television explaining this than any other issue. She didn't mind, not really, if it helped move things forward, except that it kept her away from the work itself.

These television appearances were the way they maintained widespread public support. Emma had to turn on charm at levels she wasn't aware she had, and bring some of her team members with her, but in the end it worked.

The acoustic challenge was one she could not get around. It was real, and unfortunately, unavoidable. In order to achieve the goal of deploying the sunshades in a reasonable amount of time, launches would have to happen every minute or so twenty four hours a day for an extended period of time. Every launch would create a major sonic boom. Therefore the solution was obvious. The facility would not be anywhere near a city.

The site would have to be on an island and it would have to be the only thing on that island. Only those who worked at the facility, and the necessary security forces, would occupy it. It would be an otherwise uninhabited island.

That limited the choices. It had to be an island, and it had to be near the equator, and the weather had to be amenable to supporting constant launches for a reasonable period of time.

She knew just the place.

Chapter Fourteen

The various governments had been convinced that the optimal place to locate the first launch facility was on Isla Varo, an isolated, virtually deserted island, near the equator. The island itself was not large, only about three by seven miles, but it had everything they needed. It was out of the path that most of the super storms had taken, it was not the home of an active volcano, and had no permanent human inhabitants. It was nearly perfect.

It was a few hour boat trip from Ecuador, and was within range of smaller propeller-driven airplanes for quick resupply trips. A deep-water boat dock for unloading construction supplies would have to be built, but that much was easy.

Based on the pictures of the island available on the web it was even beautiful. It seemed like a miniature home away from home for Emma who missed Tahiti. It was far enough away from any other inhabited location, so that the sonic booms would not disturb existing populations. Locations had been identified for each slingatron, the launch control center, the operations center, satellite links, onsite living quarters, and the modular nuclear power plants. It was the perfect place to build the devices that would save the planet.

***

Emma was now in the middle of another career crisis. According to her mentor, Professor Roberts, all creative scientists eventually learn that earning a higher degree is not enough. At some point, he told her, it isn't enough to create new knowledge, or discover new things. You then must put that knowledge into action and do something real with it.

For her project that wasn't the challenge. Putting theory into action, and getting people to understand what is needed to make the system work was certainly what she was doing.

The dominant motivation for the project team was that everyone on the planet felt the impact of every small delay. Every major storm meant that no matter how successful that particular day had been in making progress toward a working system, they felt they had to finish, and finish fast.

And yet there were many delays. Those delays were not caused by the lack of human ability to find scientific solutions or to engineer new machines. Making progress more difficult than technology alone. Many politicians both in the U.S. and the U.N. had formed strong negative opinions, despite the fact that many of them had little knowledge about the topic that had taken Emma a lifetime to understand. That didn't stop them from presenting themselves as qualified to decide the fate of the program, and to claim as much on any news broadcast willing to give them some air time. Most of those opposing the project were claiming that it was too costly and would have little or no impact, all without presenting any data to support their claims. Emma and Cliff were often called away from leading progress on the project to answer the latest unsubstantiated objections with real data that demonstrated the objections were wrong. It seemed as if the project was constantly on trial and guilty in the minds of many until proven innocent. The frustration this caused for the project team was that each of these exercises delayed the schedule.

This project dwarfed the size of the programs in the early days of the space race, and even the Manhattan Project. Thankfully she wasn't running the overall programmatic and management tasks for the project, but she was the scientific lead, which was hectic enough.

It meant that she lost control of her baby at the policy level, but she was grateful to turn over the details of the engineering and program management to others. For the most part it was the Program Manager and the Engineering Leads who held the day-to-day decision making power, her responsibility was limited to scientific matters. It was a comfortable role for her. Her other job was to keep the public informed, the various funding governments happy that things were progressing in a way that would solve the problem, and to ensure that there were no significant delays that couldn't be overcome.

She knew that the largest contribution she had made to the project occurred when she got the project rolling. She sold the public and decision makers on committing funding. She now held an overall system design and public relations role, and was not involved in the individual hardware details. She would remain the recognized face of the program, despite her personal preferences, because she was the one the public and politicians recognized. Her career had taken a public relations direction that she never anticipated when she began her university studies, and she had progressively less and less time for the technical details that had been the foundation of her success.

She took pride in leading the systems design task. If there was some aspect of the project that would be much easier with a detail change, it was her team that decided if the changes would impact the overall performance. She really wasn't involved in the process of doing the analysis; she was just the final authority. She had no part in managing the detailed hardware implementation, which was performed by the engineering department. But her organization set the program direction, and that was the bedrock upon which the remainder of the project would be built. The final success or failure of the program was in the hands of her team.

She learned from the engineers that with some minor changes to her initial designs, large cost or time savings could be obtained with little or no scientific impact. No one person could optimize every detail, and they had an amazing management and engineering team that was outstandingly competent.

From a scientific perspective, it was a simple concept to place the sunshades into space at the appropriate Sun-Earth Lagrange point. However, going from even a large-scale scientific proof of principle experiment to a deployed system entered an entirely different type of project-oriented discipline.

She knew that she could not fully relax until the system was operational. She felt a responsibility to the population of the Earth to implement control of the average global temperature. Once the first set of shades were in place, she would feel better, because then progress toward the goal would be tangible, it would be more real, less abstract. From that point forward it would be a "turn the crank" kind of project.

She began every day by attending a program management meeting held in the overall manager's conference room. It was a large meeting room with an elliptical table that had been heavily utilized since the very first day. Hanging on one wall were artist's concept paintings of the completed Slingatrons and buildings taking up the entirety of that wall. On the other side of the room, directly opposite from those concept illustrations, was a wall-to-wall master chart that summarized the critical events in, and timing of, the entire construction project. This wall was a mess of paper, hand written notes, lines, and various arrows all-trying to make sense of everything.

The dominant mindset, at almost every program level meeting, was construction. There was nothing on these charts, yet, about program operations or global temperature control. Those topics were reserved for meetings in the Operations Center, which occupied a completely different building.

Cliff Morris called the meeting to order in the same way every day. He had not missed a single meeting since taking the job. He told her once, over lunch, that he had no expectation of missing one until the sunshades were built, up in space, and running. Then he would retire, sit on his back porch, and read a stack of books he had been meaning to get to for years.

The Chief Engineer was a man named Savio Zdenko, an MIT graduate known for boundless energy and the ability to quickly dive into any engineering problem in any discipline brought to his attention. He was a good man and she liked working with him. He would never force a change if she could show that, according to the science, it would render the system incapable of reaching some of the goals that the project had to achieve.

The meeting room was filled to capacity every day. It was designed around the program's organizational chart. This program manager did not tolerate lack of a representative from every department, every day. There would be no empty chairs. He even had the names of the various required functional groups embroidered into the chairs so that he could see at a glance what group was missing.

He also insisted that everyone be present, and the meeting start, exactly on time. Those present must be fully prepared to report on the past twenty-four hours of progress, as well as answer any questions that were asked.

Cliff went through his usual list of announcements. These ranged from supplier issues that needed to be resolved, to a review of which critical tasks needed to be completed next in order to ensure the program stayed on schedule, and then there was his daily emphasis on safety.

Cliff had personally been involved in many government construction programs, and he had always stressed safety. This concern started when he was a child and his father had been an astronaut. He had perished along with six other astronauts in a tragic accident. The accident was eventually found to be because someone, somewhere, had not fully adhered to required safety standards. It was never going to happen on a program that he was running. There was no tolerance for error in the area of safety. He wouldn't throw in unnecessary roadblocks that slowed things down, but he also would not accept any shortcuts that jeopardized safety.

Emma felt a certain connection with him because they had both lost parents tragically. It drove them both toward being successful in their professional lives. In the case of this project, it drove them to push the system, and those funding it, to make the highest priority be the protection of human life. He would protect those who were building the system, and it was her job to protect the remainder of humanity.

In order to joke with him just a little bit, Emma had ordered child safety cushions for the corners of all rectangular tables in the main building. He got excited and said they should be used everywhere at the facility. She decided that program managers had no discernable sense of humor, and never tried another joke after that.

Their largest safety problem in this program was the launch process. Whenever objects move at the velocity at which the payloads would exit the slingatron, there was an inherent risk. Emma never tried to hide that from anyone. This would be the first program to actively use many of these technologies outside of a science laboratory.

For instance, it was a first to operationally deploy large inflatable structures that would be in a liquid state prior to UV curing in space. Previous inflatables had been made from a flexible material whose rigidity came from the inflation pressure rather than from hardening the material.

This had been demonstrated in a laboratory vacuum chamber at Physical Sciences, Inc. a few years after the turn of the century but that was a far more controlled environment. She had even deployed proof of principle bubbles in low earth orbit. But to then take them to the Lagrange point and operate them under control from the ground was a pioneering endeavor.

The proof of principle had sent un-inflated liquid material into low earth orbit. There the material was inflated in the Earth's shadow. The ultraviolet portion of the solar spectrum cured the inflated bubble when it emerged into the sunlight. In the vacuum of space, the interior pressure of the bubble could be very much lower for inflation than would have been required for a balloon or any other shape in the atmosphere.

The full-scale sunshade project took this one step further. Rather than inflating spherical bubbles, flat structures would be made using expanding circular rings that rely on surface tension of the liquid to adhere to the structure during expansion. Then, like the demonstration bubbles before them, the full size flat sunshades would cure in solar ultraviolet light after emerging from the Earth's shadow. The flat structures needed even less launch payload volume than a sphere to reach the same size. After the completed structure was fully cured, it would be raised to the LaGrange point using an electric propulsion booster. Once in place in their final orbit, the amount of shading could be controlled by tilting the flat sunshade. A television journalist called it a giant Venetian blind system.

Savio had completely simulated all of the steps that had never before been done. That simulation showed that the overall risk of the Earth orbit deployment and ferrying of the sunshades to the Lagrange point was lower than many of the other tasks on the program, and lower than any of the other concepts for inserting the sunshades into the correct location in space.

Savio had also simulated an advantage of the special sunshade material developed specifically for this program. The non-brittle cured solid material would mean that the replacement rate of the deployed sunshades due to meteoroid impacts would be surprisingly low. The holes would be very small compared to the size of the structures themselves. Therefore the lifetime of any particular sunshade was expected to significantly exceed the originally anticipated longevity, and that meant operational cost savings. They would still have to be replaced after a certain amount of operating time, but that time would be longer than originally expected.

Savio was much more concerned with the Slingatron launch system. It had been invented in the previous century. It had never been used in a major application, and before the decision to use it for the sunshade project, it was not widely known outside of the small group of people who strongly supported the operational principle.

Emma had come across the concept in graduate school. She was instantly won over by the simple physics. She understood that it had the potential to launch large numbers of payloads into orbit in short periods of time.

At the time, she found it fascinating that as a child she had unknowingly used the same gyrational acceleration principle to launch marbles across a room. It was something that annoyed her father, but it greatly amused the three-year old Emma for a few months. It was one of her earliest memories.

She had a circular container that was perhaps ten inches in diameter. She would take the lid off of the container, and use a single marble as her projectile. She would place the marble in the lid and move it in a gyrating motion. To her surprise the marble would come out much faster than her motion. She would later understand, while in graduate school, that it would be moving ten times faster than her gyrations if she had been using a one-inch motion and if it was indeed a ten-inch lid. She thought it was great. Her father really didn't like the dents in the sheetrock walls, so she eventually learned to shoot them into curtains, but she loved the shooting.

While she was in prep school she had dated someone

whose behavior had disappointed her. She had shot marbles at pictures of him in this same way. At the time she found it to be very stress relieving.

When she first learned about the slingatron concept, she read as many of Derek Tidman's writings as she could. He and his collaborators really understood the potential of this concept.

Frictional losses and motor drive inefficiencies were the only physical processes that caused less than one hundred percent of the applied electrical power from being converted to kinetic energy of the payload.

As she headed out the door to walk to the morning meeting, she was glad to be working with the team they had assembled for this project. They would get very difficult and very large things done.

***

The morning meeting had been predictable and without surprise. They were preparing for a major test and Cliff was enthusiastic. This was an orbital launch test of the Slingatron, one they had been anticipating for weeks.

Previous testing had shown the ability to achieve five kilometers per second velocities with a ten-kilogram payload. That payload had included a small booster rocket that accelerated a one-half kilogram nanosatellite to slightly less than eight kilometers per second so that it entered the low earth orbit they desired.

The press had, predictably, chided the massively expensive program for being happy about a 1957 Sputnik level of technological achievement. However, Cliff had insisted to every reporter who managed to reach him on the phone that the performance of every aspect of the Slingatron test was successful. The test was actually well beyond that of Sputnik, he insisted, because they had successfully launched eleven of these satellites in a thirteen minute time span, and that had never before been done. More importantly, all of the payloads achieved orbit, and there was no measurable deterioration of the Slingatron launch tube.

Today's test would demonstrate a nine-kilometer per second exit from the Slingatron. With a high launch elevation angle, the velocity after atmospheric frictional losses would still be sufficient to achieve low earth orbit. No rocket power would be needed to achieve earth orbital velocity. Small divert thrusters would be carried so that the insertion angles could be altered once the payload was out of the atmosphere. This was a very important test because of the higher velocity, and it would also serve as a test of the new ablative coatings on the payloads. One coating ablated inside the slingatron itself to create a gas bearing so that payload actually was not in direct contact with the rails. The other coating ablated during the brief interval that the payload passed through the atmosphere.

Launch countdowns had always seemed overly dramatic to Emma. However, she had come to appreciate all of the various go-no-go conditions that had to be met during the time approaching a launch.

Each of these decisions had to be made at a specific time.

Countdowns did serve one purpose. She could not help feeling an emotional response at various milestones in the timeline, because more items were cleared for launch. The failure of any one of those items could either delay or stop a launch, and cause expensive delays in the overall program. Her inner scientist still found some of those milestones rather like grandstanding for some of the simple functions being checked. She thought that maybe she had just watched too many of them, and there had never been a failure in any of the previous systems tests.

At every test, Savio would hover over first one, then another, of several workstations as he paced back and forth. His pacing was part nervousness and part useful observation of each station he passed.

Cliff was always the most composed at these tests. He had put everything he had into preparation to get here, and now he depended on his team to execute their jobs appropriately.

She knew, as did Cliff and Savio, that history was being made. If everything being said about the acceleration of climate change was correct, then the well being of mankind itself was on the line. If they were successful, history would remember this project and those working on this project positively. If they failed, there could be serious consequences and millions of people might not survive.

The countdown had dipped into the single digits. Emma watched the video monitor and stopped watching the timer.

If she had continued to watch the timer, she might have preferred it. The timer never reached zero. At one second to launch the payload making its way through to the end of the Slingatron exited the side of the launch tube rather than the end. It flew straight at the Launch Control Center moving at seven kilometers per second, and the fifty-kilogram payload released what would later be calculated to be twelve hundred MegaJoules of energy as it penetrated the exterior wall. That was the same amount of kinetic energy as a Boeing 747 just before takeoff.

***

Straight was sitting far from his lobbying office in Washington DC. He was in his father's living room when they saw the news. The launch failure was worldwide news immediately. He noticed that his father did not seem surprised and merely smirked at the news. He wondered if those trying to project Mother Nature from mankind's purposeful manipulation were behind this failure.

***

The fallout from the test failure was much worse than Emma expected. Yes, the press was accurate when it called the energy release "over a quarter ton of TNT." It had been accurately reported on the news that she had not been able to suppress a scream when the Control Center was hit. The damage was relatively minor compared to the expectations generated by the enormous noise level and dust cloud. None of that stopped many of those in the launch facility from having nightmares for weeks afterwards.

The Slingatron was not so lucky. It had suffered surprisingly expensive damage. The destruction required more than one hundred million dollars, and worse, several months, to repair. But, before repairs could begin, there were months of root cause analysis from a large number of external reviewers that she, Savio, Cliff, and the entire team had to endure.

The failure analysis caused a five-month delay before repair and ultimately construction could begin again. She was overjoyed that the flaw had not been a flaw in the architecture that would have been the end of the program, and perhaps a significant fraction of mankind. Some faulty equipment had caused it from one of the contractors. They blamed something in their assembly line, but it didn't matter. The end result was they failed to do their job, and delay was the result. Mankind didn't have time for this sort of thing.

Some people thought that the delay was going to be catastrophic.

Many people had feared that would be the case. There had even been a spike in the sales of survival equipment when the press had announced their failed test. She knew there would not be any way to hide from the climate change that was coming if they failed. While the program was shut down for failure analysis, she was on television every day giving updates to anyone who would listen. She spent her days in makeup chairs preparing for these appearances, and dodging protestors who were now growing in numbers, including some people called Nature First. They were the worst. They thought that purposefully manipulating nature was the height of arrogance.

It had been determined that the problem was in one of the divert rocket thrusters that had been part of the payload. It had come loose and damaged the launch tube. This caused the payload to penetrate and exit in "an unplanned way" from the Slingatron, the final report said.

It may have been unplanned and a minor setback in principle, but to Emma it was a lost year. A year she didn't think they could afford to lose.

Now that the program was back up and running, she had a wedding to plan, and her first vacation in far too long.

Chapter Fifteen

Emma looked at herself in the mirror, and reality finally smacked her between the eyes. By the end of the day she would be married. She had known it ever since Scott asked her to be his wife, and that was almost eighteen months ago. Somehow it hadn't seemed real until just that moment looking at her reflection in a wedding dress.

She had worn it before, but today it seemed different. Perhaps it was because she hadn't really done much of the planning. Work had kept her so busy that most of the time she could barely keep track of the day of the week, so the wedding planning had been farmed out to others.

When Scott had first asked her the big question, she had said yes without any hesitation. In fact, she hadn't realized until the instant he asked just how much she wanted to take that step in life. Three weeks later he brought up the subject of a date and they both sighed at the thought of all the planning, and the challenge of finding a spare week or two on both of their schedules simultaneously for a wedding plus honeymoon.

She had seen the evolving details of this day as the wedding planner had sent them to her during the weeks leading up to this event, but it had all seemed so abstract. It had looked like some of the early mock ups her mom used to get for future movie sets. It had all seemed so unreal before today.

The wedding planner himself was a celebrity guest list event specialist from California. This would be one of those events. That embarrassed her, but her public profile put certain demands on parts of her life. She argued vehemently that she would prefer to just elope, but that was not possible. She tried to talk Scott into it two or three different times. She even threatened to get him drunk in Las Vegas when they were there for a conference, and take him to a wedding chapel. But he pointed out that the politics of her job would create a long list of influential people wanting to claim that they had been at her wedding. So here she was, in a one of a kind designer dress, looking at herself while thinking that it looked a little silly, yet she liked it at the same time.

The event would take place at a church in Beverly Hills, California, with a reception at a nearby country club. She had wanted a honeymoon in the tropics, but the unpredictable weather motivated them instead to rent a beach house for a week in Malibu, just north of Los Angeles. They wanted to be close to a major airport if a large storm headed their way. One perk of their job was that they would hear about it first, and receive enough warning to, hopefully, get on a flight out of town. She didn't like to ask for special treatment, but her job was to bring these storms to an end, so she had to be available.

The guest list meant that they would have media representatives waiting outside to try to catch glimpses of some world leader or other, as well as the many celebrities who would be in attendance. The Tahitian girl in her would have preferred twenty close friends on the beach, instead of the four hundred VIP guests they had coming, but it was too late to make that dream into a reality.

The cost of the day had been insane, and she really had wished for the informal low-key event that had been her girlhood dream. But then she saw herself in the dress and she knew that this was something that she would remember forever. She had to admit that she was secretly happy they had done it this way.

She came back to reality with a knock on the door, "Hello," she called.

"Emma, hey it's me, are you ready?" her maid of honor asked.

When the wedding planning started, she could not think of a single close friend who she could ask to fulfill that role. She chose instead to go with a friend of her mother's who had been a sounding board for many years as emotional issues arose. Their age was different by two decades but Emma felt closer to her than to any friends her own age.

Emma was greatly amused to watch Scott's father around some of the actresses he revered. Many of them had retired from the hectic life of an actor, but he remembered them as they had appeared on-screen, and occasionally he would be caught open-mouthed but speechless. They were used to it. Emma found it highly entertaining.

She had arranged a practical joke for him at the reception, five specific theme songs would be played in a row, and five very carefully chosen actresses would each ask him to dance. Her mother-in-law-to-be was in on it, and had helped to choose the list. She couldn't wait to see how he reacted. What was life without a little fun? Scott's father would never forget this day, she would make sure of that.

Both Scott and his parents gave every outward appearance of their joy at this event that would join him to Emma for a lifetime. Few people at this event knew that Scott's brother, his parent's only other son, would not attend because he had died in the super storm that devastated London. Emma knew that they would never mention it at this event. It was a time for happiness.

The door opened and her friend told her, "You really do look like your mother. Perhaps you are a little younger than she was when I first met her, but you do have her figure, and the resemblance just can't be missed. If this whole 'save the planet science thing' ever gets boring, you give me a call. We will get you some auditions."

"That's ok, I would be terrible. I can't get emotional on cue, and who can remember all those lines anyway," she said between laughter.

"They make these things called cue cards and I know you can read," came the sarcastic reply.

"Ok, I'm ready. I guess we should go, then maybe I can get out of these shoes later, my gosh these things hurt, but look fantastic," Emma said.

They walked from the bride's dressing room to the main church.

Normally someone would walk the bride down the aisle, but she didn't feel comfortable with anyone other than her father, so she walked alone. She walked into the room and everyone stood as the traditional wedding march reverberated throughout the chapel.

The chapel was decorated more beautifully than she could have imagined. She asked for something that reminded her of home. They had filled the place with flowers that she had only ever seen in Tahiti. They were so rare elsewhere else that she was very surprised to see them. The place was filled with orange, red, blue, and purple blooms, the exotic curves of tropical petals, green leaves, and smells that reminded her of home. She had really missed all of it. Work had been so dominant in her life that she rarely thought about it. Now she wished she could fly backward in time and spend more of her life there instead of off at school. She realized that she was nervous. She wasn't nervous about the marriage, it was the event that gave her butterflies.

As she made her way toward the front, she felt less nervous with every step. The man she loved was there, and they would spend the rest of their lives together. It didn't matter if she tripped going up the aisle, the end result would be the same. They would be married.

When she got the sunshades up and running, they could spend more time with each other. Perhaps they could even move back to the South Pacific if the climate returned to the way it used to be. Well, she thought, that was her home and not his, but perhaps they could spend some time there at least.

She brought her mind back to the events of the day

as the Priest went through the ceremony. Her part was easy. It seemed like this was so quick. She couldn't believe all the preparation it had taken to get to this day for a fifteen-minute ceremony. It seemed almost anti-climactic in a way. But there it was, her one line, Scott had already said his.

"I do," she said.

"You may kiss the bride," the priest said.

She leaned in to kiss him. They had kissed many times before, but this one was different. It was electric. It was a starting point for the rest of their lives.

With that kiss, they were married, and loud cheers arose from the festive audience. The crowd of relatives, friends, political luminaries, famous actors, and assorted posers all seemed genuinely elated. Perhaps the champagne helped.

They walked back up the aisle. She was smiling ear-to-ear, as was Scott. It was liberating in a way. Now she had almost everything she had ever dreamed about, and more. Only when she was very little did she dream of the day she would marry. But since turning fourteen, she had been so independent that she rarely thought about it. She would have never considered it before Scott. But here she was...married.

Before she knew it, she was in the limousine and being whisked away from the church toward the reception hall.

"Oh my God, we finally did it," she said to Scott.

"Yes we did. Who knew we would find the time in our lives, but we finally did it Doctor," he joked using her professional title.

"What do we do now?" she joked.

"Well I guess we go on a vacation, whatever that is," he said with a wink.

"Oh that's right, you have no idea how to relax near the Ocean. That's ok. I grew up on an island; let me be your guide," she joked.

"I guess I will have to trust you, but remember I burn quickly with too much sun," he said.

"Well, you see, there is something called sunscreen, some chemist invented it a while ago. You should think about experiments more than theory once in a while." she said sarcastically as she kissed him again, this time deeper than before.

It was not a long drive from the chapel to the reception and they arrived before anyone. They went inside to change into something far more comfortable, at least from the perspective of her shoes. She never understood how some women wore these balancing act shoes all day and into the night.

The reception also had a Tahitian theme, right down to the food and small details like wall photographs that had been changed in favor of scenes from her home island, before the storms. There was a beach barbeque in the back with fruit and decorations, all from home. They had mangos, dragon fruit, two roast pigs, a dance floor, and a band that could have been cut straight out of an old Tahitian tourism ad. It was perfect. The whole thing brought tears to her eyes.

The guests started to arrive. The place was packed with everyone from the Vice President of the United States representing the President, to last year's Best Actor Oscar Winner. Emma was enjoying a cocktail, chatting, and watching her father-in-law try to dance with an actress and form a coherent sentence at the same time. It was the night of her life…until someone tapped her on the shoulder.

"Doctor Hallbar, I hate to interrupt, can I speak to you for a moment?" said a man she had never met.

"Sure, I don't think we have ever met," she said extending her hand. There were so many people who brought guests with them that there were many people here whom she had never met, so it wasn't unusual.

"I'm one of the people you suckered into allowing my tax dollars to go to pay for your useless sunshades to fight a made up problem that isn't real. How can someone be so arrogant as to think they can purposefully alter Mother Nature's plan," he started dragging her towards an exit.

"What? SECURITY," she shouted.

Her heart was racing; she had no idea what to do. Scott grabbed the man and tried to free her.

Since the Vice President was in the room, Secret Service agents were everywhere. She should not have worried, but she panicked. She couldn't breathe.

The agents were there immediately. They quickly removed the man from Scott's grasp, freed Emma, and two agents rushed the man out the back door quickly. Four other agents flanked Scott and Emma and rushed them out the front door before they knew what happened. They were placed quickly into the Vice President's bulletproof limousine.

Emma was catching her breath in the back seat. She looked at Scott, "Who was that guy?"

She hadn't realized an agent made it into the vehicle with them.

"He came in with one of the guests. His name, as we were given it, is Sebastian Moran, but that is almost surely an alias. No matter, you are safe here and the local police have additional units en-route to take him out of here." We will get you back inside once we secure the facility. It won't take long," the male agent said.

"Thank you agent. I'm sorry I don't know your name and now I wish I did. Why was he trying to get me out the door?" she asked.

"My name is Frank ma'am. We think he wanted to do you harm but we had secured the reception hall as weapon free as it could possibly be. No matter, we have him in custody. He will not get anywhere close to you again," he said.

"Thank you Frank," it was then that the agent handed Emma a phone.

"Ma'am it's the President on the line," he said.

"How...Ok," she took the phone.

"Mr. President, thank you for calling," she said assuming this was for congratulations.

"Emma, I heard what happened. I want you to know that I am going to assign a Secret Service detail to you and your husband for the time being until we sort out what is going on," he said.

"Mr. President, I'm sure that isn't necessary," she said.

"I'm afraid I insist. I'm also sorry to say that you will not enjoy having this level of security, but better safe than sorry. Also, there is a storm coming to the East Coast so I'm being evacuated to the West Coast. Apparently it is huge. But please do not cancel your honeymoon. I just talked to the Program Manager at the Slingatron Project and he assures me everything is on schedule. Your deputy is doing a wonderful job. He sounded a little bit stressed out since you have never been away before, although it is quite possible that the stress could just have been because no one warned him I was calling. When you get back, I want you and the various teams to work on how to speed things along. We need the fix sooner rather than later, and to hell with the cost overrun. The estimates on this newest storm are a hundred thousand people will either be displaced, injured, or killed, and there is nothing I can do about it except clean up the mess afterwards. I'm tired of the pounding, and we need it to end," he said.

"Yes, Mr. President. Thank you for calling," she said and turned to kiss her husband as her racing heartbeat began to return to normal. The combination of the wedding, the attempted attack, and concern about the east coast storm had elevated her blood pressure and brought a rosy flush to her cheeks.

She knew she would have a difficult time relaxing on their honeymoon now, but she was determined to try.

Chapter Sixteen

After their honeymoon Emma had returned to work. With dedication, hard work and intense effort the launch system was finally up, the slingatron facility was finally working. The team was placing equipment into orbit on a regular basis, and the sunshades were being put in place. Everything she worked toward on her quest to normalize the climate the planet was happening, and ahead of schedule.

Emma had more than just professional success in her life. She had big news to share with Scott. He was flying in to join her at the island, and his flight was late. It was not unusual for that to happen, the facility had no access other than by boat and chartered seaplane. He was going to come in with the latest supply of food. That way there was no need to charter a special flight.

They had been married for a few months now, and while they had not been consciously trying to have a baby, she was pregnant. When she had found out she thought it wasn't possible, there must be some mistake, but it made her happy beyond words. While it was difficult not to tell him immediately, she wanted to deliver this bit of news in person. This was not something for their daily video chats.

She checked with the port director who doubled as the air traffic controller, and it would be at least another hour before the plane arrived. Since the Slingatron was down for routine maintenance checks, she decided to take the time during this break from the constant sonic booms to take a walk out on the beach. It was hard not to enjoy the sound of the waves breaking on the shore combined with the smell of the salt air. Growing up on Tahiti had imprinted her with that combination.

As Emma walked through the gate, the Sergeant working security there asked her to be careful, and to make sure that she kept her phone, which doubled as a location-tracking device, with her just in case she needed anything. Whoever was guarding the gate urged the same type of caution every time anyone went out for a stroll. So far the worst thing that had happened outside the gate was a sprained ankle. She went without a second thought, but was polite to the man and said she would be sure to be careful, and even held her phone up so he could see it.

As she made her way to the beach, she saw a large ship off shore. That wasn't unusual, the launch facility had become a bit of a tourist attraction. Large charter boats came by the island once in a while to get a glimpse of the place and take pictures, hopefully while a launch was happening. Boats were required to have arranged clearance in advance to approach within a three-mile limit. They even arranged tour groups during maintenance breaks from time to time so they could approach the island more closely. She assumed this one was waiting for the maintenance to finish so the launches would begin again and they could take some pictures, then the passengers could claim they had seen one for themselves.

Something about this ship didn't seem the same as

the others. She couldn't put her finger on what it was, but she kept walking and glanced at it from time to time as she continued her walk. She didn't stare at it, but in the back of her mind she was trying to decide exactly what was different about this one.

Emma was about to dismiss it as just her mind playing tricks on her, when she gave it another glance. That was when she saw the large ship launching several smaller vessels. She had seen this happen near Tahiti often enough. Sometimes smaller boats would come ashore from super yachts that were too large to get in the more shallow waters near shore. She had never seen that happen this close to the launch facility, and she had no idea why they were doing this. It didn't fit the pattern.

Suddenly from the single port facility on the island, the military contingent was sending a small, but quick, boat out to intercept them and turn them away. It wasn't that visitors were unwelcome, but there were dangerous things on the island and their safety could not be guaranteed. Only visitors with appointments were allowed in, and the waiting list was very long. It appeared these boats had no such appointment. She looked toward the compound and noticed some of the uniformed military starting to scurry about.

She was turning back when she heard some strange noises coming across the water. She couldn't place them and had to think for a second but she quickly realized what it was. Gunfire...it couldn't be anything else. She did not want to believe it at first, so she looked back to the water, hoping for some other explanation.

But there was no mistaking it. The launched vessels were firing on the military intercept. The single small craft that had been launched from the island had three military members on it and only one weapon. It tried to turn and come back to the island as one of the crew made an attempt to man the one weapon mounted to the deck, but it was too late. She watched as all three men on board fell over the side into the water with a splash that could only be made by an uncontrolled landing. She knew what people jumping in the water looked like, and they were not jumping, they were in pain or dead based on how twisted they were as they dropped over the side. They had been taken by surprise and had no time to react. She did not see them come up.

Emma stood there in disbelief. How could this be happening? Her heart was racing.

Didn't everyone know the good they were trying to do here? The facility had been criticized by conspiracy theorists claiming that the scientists were faking the data. There had been the wacko who made his way into their wedding somehow. These people said that the storms were just part of ordinary weather fluctuations, that it was all part of Mother Nature's plan. She knew that it was not possible to convince everyone. Not everyone would understand the chaotic science involved in planetary climates. But to launch an attack?

The boats were coming closer, and coming in unbelievably fast. She ran back towards the gate as fast as she could. She kept looking back. They were so fast... the military inside the gate was scrambling and alarms started going off everywhere.

The boats were, at most, two hundred meters from shore now and coming in quickly.

How could they be that fast on water? Even in panic mode her overactive brain began to list the possibilities: hydrofoils, ground effect airborne boats, hovercraft, actively controlled hydroplanes that no longer flipped over.

She was almost at the gate. If she could just get inside, she knew she would be much safer. The military inside the fence was getting into the positions she had seem them use during drills. She had never imagined she would see them do this against a real attack, and always thought the drills were just to give them something to do.

She focused all of her attention on the gate and those all-important defenses as she ran. The alarms suddenly stopped and everything was so quiet...but how could that be?

She looked toward the power plant and saw some black clad men moving around. They didn't belong there, and she realized they must have cut the power lines. She feared that all of the technology used to keep the island safe would now be useless! It was all so high tech that it had to have power.

Suddenly those men in black were being met by the onsite military. Shots were fired in both directions, and the ones who didn't belong fell to the ground. The military was far more accurate with their weaponry.

All the noise stopped. It was so silent that it made her heart beat speed up more than she ever thought it could, the fear level continued rise, and adrenaline continued to pour into her veins. She was ten meters away with a sergeant waving her in and running towards her while keeping his weapon pointed at something behind her. Suddenly the Sergeant fired a few times. She kept running.

Then she could hear more weapons being fired. An explosion behind her broke the silence. She was thrown to the ground. She saw the sergeant continuing to fire over her head at something.

She crawled with everything she had, trying to get through that gate. The sergeant grabbed her hand and started pulling. She felt something warm running down her leg and there was a searing pain.

"Doctor Hallbar, stay with me. You have been shot, but it isn't bad. It is only a flesh wound; you are bleeding, and a medic will be here in just a few seconds. Stay low," the man shouted.

"Shot! How could I have been shot?" she looked at her leg. Blood was streaking down her formerly white pants. They were now brown from the dirt and increasingly red from the blood. Her heart beat faster, and she started to panic. She could hear someone yelling for a medic. She could no longer tell who was who and where the noises were coming from.

More military men were running around. She couldn't tell which way the facility was, and which way was the beach. Suddenly there was a man in front of her. She recognized from his insignia that he was a combat medic

"Doctor Hallbar, my name is Emmit. I am going to stop the bleeding. You are safe right here, but until we can stop the bleeding I don't want to move you. The fighting isn't near us at the moment. They have been pushed back down on the beach, so don't worry," he said trying to keep her calm while working as quickly as he could.

He gave her an injection of something. She barely noticed what he did after that. He was doing something to her leg but she felt no pain.

She moved her head around trying to get her bearings. She finally determined where the sounds originated.

Down on the beach, she could see through the haze in her vision that the U.S. Military contingent was moving in defined formations towards some people running up the beach. The automated defenses were still working but she didn't understand how with the power cut.

There was some exchange of gunfire back and forth. It was a one sided slaughter. The men coming on the beach were firing quickly but not terribly accurately. The military group from the facility was far more accurate.

She watched as more men on the beach fell to the ground, some clutching an arm, some clutching a leg.

She watched as one was running closer to the fence and toward the gate.

Someone with an automatic weapon opened fire on him. His head disappeared and was replaced with what looked like a side of beef, mangled as holes appeared first in the front, then larger in the back. What she could only assume was brain matter was lying on the paved roadway in small grey gelatinous chunks next to some stark white skull fragments. She thought she saw some of his hair still clinging to a patch of skin half on and half off a larger piece of skull bone.

She lost consciousness with that image in her eyes.

***

Emma woke up in an office on a couch. Scott was beside her, holding her hand.

"What happened?" she asked putting a hand to her forehead trying to get her bearings.

"You are fine. You were shot in the leg. It put a small hole, nicked was the term the doctor used, in an artery but they got everything closed up quickly. You were very lucky," he said weakly. He was having trouble keeping himself from losing it.

"Who were they?" she asked, not sure if it mattered.

"A mercenary group hired by someone. We don't know who hired them yet," he said.

"Why?" she asked.

"We have no idea. Aren't you glad we kept the military presence on the island now?" he asked.

"Yeah, I have to agree that was smart. But I still don't get it, we are trying to save the planet here. What was it they hoped to accomplish?" she asked.

"Some people don't see it that way. There are some organizations that think no one should mess with the environment even if you are doing so beneficially. Those Mother Nature first people we keep hearing about. I was starting to think they were just a myth until that guy showed up at our wedding. There are others who do this sort of thing in the name of religion. They think God should solve whatever problems the earth faces. Then there are just people who want to be in control of the system once it is up, maybe to hold the world ransom. Who knows, someday you can explain to me why you gave your Secret Service detail the morning off, they are supposed to be with you all the time," he said.

"Scott...I am sorry, and I had to work hard to convince them it was ok. I also told them I wouldn't go outside the gate, and therefore I would be under the protection of the military but...I had wanted this to be a great day, I have some news, and I hope nothing is wrong, and that it is still good news..." she took a deep breath. She hoped her injury didn't do anything to hurt her pregnancy.

"You're pregnant, I know, the doctor told me and the baby is fine," he said, a tear in his eye.

"Oh thank God," she sat up and hugged him as hard as she ever had, now that she had found the ability to move a little. She realized she was in her office. "Why am I in my office? Shouldn't I be in the medical unit?" she asked.

"It is a small unit, with just one doctor, and there were a lot of wounded," he said.

She had never even thought about that. She had not thought about the aftermath of the battle.

"How many were killed?" she asked closing her eyes because part of here did not want to know, and she hoped it was not many.

"Just one of our contingent. On their side the number is unknown. It turns out the ship they had out in the water was pretty well armed with very large caliber field artillery weapons similar in design to those used during the World War, and started shooting at the facility. Our military shot back with a single missile and their boat is now a giant mess out in the water. We don't know how many they lost," he said.

"How is the launch system, was there any damage?" she realized was speaking very quickly.

"They managed to get some divers ashore to cut the power line from the power plant to the facility, but they didn't know the military had their own power source. I think they were counting on our forces being without power. The weapon systems and the slingatron all have their own independent and redundant power plants for security and reliability. As you know, that fact was never made public. The slingatron and control system are fine. Once the physical plant power is fixed, everything will be back up and running normally," he said.

"Scott we have to get this thing running and move on. If we can get all of the sunshades up, and fix the climate, then I want to retire. Just live our lives in peace," she said not sure if she believed it.

He pulled her close hugging her tightly, "I'm there…"

"I love you," she said into his shoulder as she started to cry.

Chapter Seventeen

Emma stood on her balcony looking out at the beautiful water. One of the unexpected perks found on Varo Island was that from her family's apartment it was possible to see the sunrise and the sunset from the same chair.

She still had dreams about the attack on the island, and the group calling themselves Mother Nature's Defenders, but they weren't as often as they once were.

The villas were set upon a hilltop that gave a view of the slingatron and the payload preparation buildings. In the distance, through the trees, it was also possible to see the launch control center if you knew just where to look.

Life was not as peaceful here as she would like. There were continuous acoustic assaults upon the ears from the supersonic payloads exiting the launch system. Everyone on the island had become used to wearing earplugs, even when indoors. Those who came here for the first time usually had trouble sleeping the first few days, but once you got used to it things weren't that bad.

They had developed a type of headset hearing protector that was combined with electronic earphones and external microphones so that people could carry on a conversation while filtering out the larger noise pollution. Your body would still feel the vibrations from the sonic booms, but over time everyone had learned to ignore that. She even found that when she left the island that she felt something was missing for the first few days when she tried to fall asleep. It was too peaceful back on the mainland, until she re-acclimated to the lack of sonic booms.

Emma, and everyone on the island, really tried to make the most of the rare moments when there was nothing being hurled into space. Most of the time, there were multiple sonic booms per hour.

This island hosted all of the subsystems that challenged human tolerance. As a result, the command and control facility, or CCF that controlled both station keeping and the amount of sunlight passing through the part of the sunshade system in final orbit, were located elsewhere. The CCF was continuously populated with human operators, and it was not only better for the people, but far less expensive to keep those facilities elsewhere.

All of the command and control was located in a hardened facility located far underground at Mount Imperium in Switzerland. Within that mountain were several control rooms, each one containing multiple displays and operator interfaces.

Each of those control rooms had a different function, with redundancies scattered throughout. One was dedicated to the measurement of earth's insolation from the harsh sun, others to weather monitoring and short-range prediction around the globe, and some to long-term climate modeling. The most critical operation in that facility was station keeping and control of the physically very large, but low-mass solar shades. Even without the operators in those rooms, the system could operate autonomously in a gracefully degrading way for up to one year, but fully autonomous operation carried many risks. Human judgment was essential in order to accurately modulate the greenhouse effect.

The system had been functioning for years now, but sustained maintenance launches were still required. There were not as many launches now as there had been when the system was undergoing initial deployment, but every mechanical system ever constructed has to be maintained.

Stable thermal control was becoming an accepted part of life on planet Earth. There were children now entering elementary school who had not been alive when the super storms were common occurrences. They would only learn of them in history books.

There was a monthly report that was widely covered by the press, summarized by giving the year that had historically been characterized by the current average temperature of the Earth.

Emma took great pride in the fact that in the current year of 2050, if this system were not functioning, sea level would have risen more than a meter above the present elevation. The current climate equivalent was 2020 give or take two years.

Most news coverage still incorrectly stated that this project was directly controlling the climate. No matter how many times she explained it, they would fail to make the distinction, but that was ok. In reality, they were controlling the overall amount of global heat. The climate was changing back to being less chaotic as a direct result of that thermal control, just as they predicted. It was an energy problem. They were reducing the energy entering the global weather system, thereby favorably affecting the climate.

The chosen solution to the problem had been explained more times than anyone involved with the project would have ever thought possible. There were two choices to control the Earth's average temperature. They could either reduce greenhouse gas emissions to a pre-twenty-first century level, or they could control the solar heating experienced by the Earth. The first option had been tried, but was only marginally successful, as well as expensive. When the consequences of failure to control global warming started to mount up, it became less expensive to shade the sunlight than to continue on the historical path. It bothered her in some ways that it really did become primarily about the money, but they were saving lives by putting the sunshades in place, and that brought her peace of mind.

The overall result was exactly as predicted. Severe storms had reduced in frequency and the sea level stabilized.

Many people on the planet assumed that global temperature control by shading was now a normal part of their lives and would remain so forever. However, greenhouse gas emissions were destined to someday decline in response to the rise of sustainable energy sources. The sunshade program could easily reduce the amount of shading in the future if appropriate. That was the beauty of this solution. It could adapt as the environment changed.

However, many believed that controlling overheating of the Earth due to currently predicted greenhouse gas emissions wasn't enough. Through geologic time, the Earth had gone through multiple cold periods, including ice ages. Causes ranged from eruptions of super-volcanoes or large sets of ordinary volcanoes within a time interval of several years, to the influence of the Earth's orbit around the sun on insolation that contributed to ice age formation. There were also many other cooling threats that could affect the economy and human health at a cataclysmic level, including asteroid impacts and nuclear winter. The list was a long one.

The team on the project was confident they had control of global heating. And if a cooling period occurred, they could reduce or stop the shading of sunlight. The temperature would drop if the cooling effect was large, but no superstorms would happen. There was even a solution to global cooling events. With some thought, the team believed that anything Mother Nature decided to throw their way could be controlled.

Models of ice age formation predicted how and when the next ice age was expected to occur. In order to prevent the ice age, computer simulations showed that they had to have more leverage on the global heat budget. The modeling results were clear. It would be necessary to increase the greenhouse gas concentration in the atmosphere significantly if ice age prevention was added to the program task list.

That way the sunshades could modulate the sunlight

with enough dynamic range to prevent ice ages while maintaining the desired year 2020 thermal equilibrium. It was an interesting thought to put humans in charge instead of Mother Nature, but politically it was too much and too soon. Many things about that idea did not sit well with some people. Preventing Ice Ages would not be added to the charter of the sunshade project team.

Simulations also showed that this greenhouse gas increase, when coupled with sunshade controls, could be used to avert other natural and man-made disasters as well. At one level of greenhouse gas above that which was now present in the atmosphere, ice ages could be avoided. At another, even higher level of greenhouse gases, the after-effects of a super volcano, asteroid impact, or nuclear winter could be mitigated.

A comprehensive summary study was done that concluded that the probability of any one global event from an asteroid impact to nuclear winter was small. But the total overall risk was large enough that many advocated preparing our dynamic range of global thermal control to include heating the planet through added greenhouse gases, to solve global cooling threats. Now that overheating was no longer a threat, human ambition grew to include a desire to eliminate cooling as a threat.

If this enhanced level of control of the greenhouse effect was implemented, then governmental policy and regulations on greenhouse gas emission controls would need to be relaxed or eliminated. Many industries favored this approach and claimed they had known better all along. In addition, in the long run, the world would need new sources of these gasses. A series of artificial greenhouse gas enhancement facilities was proposed for the purpose of supplying the needed greenhouse effect. One astrophysicist called it, "Terraforming the Ice Age Earth." Work that had been done to devise ways to Terraform Mars were now being modified to apply to the home planet itself.

If greenhouse gas emission was increased, then it was obvious that in order to maintain Climate 2020, they would need a larger set of sunshades. Now that the climate was under control, and this wasn't something that was necessary to do in a hurry, it had been seriously proposed to perform these tasks gradually on a disciplined schedule. Maintenance of Climate 2020, as the press called it, would require more sunshade launches than needed for maintenance of the existing system, but that was a straightforward process involving scheduling and additional copies of currently deployed systems using demonstrated existing technological capability.

Many, including Emma in a rare time of agreeing with some of the protestors, actively advised against this process of artificial increases of the greenhouse gasses. To her, it seemed to be like playing God. This was not something humankind should do. Her motivation had always been to fix the warming that was responsible for her parent's death, not to increase the scope of the program. She viewed the proposed scope increases with great suspicion that it was motivated more to increase the power held by the project leaders, or profits of industry, than by concern for human welfare.

Many on the team rejoiced that they achieved success in time for another amazing human scientific discovery. There had been some recent advances in age reversing drugs. Some called it the fountain of youth. One could expect to live a long time in good health, and to be able to watch the planet live in the utopia that she played a major role in creating. Doctors were telling her that with modern medicine, anyone could easily live in peak health for more than two hundred years. Doctor Hallbar looked forward to every single one of them.

***

The scenery at this beach held both the most beauty and the most emotional attachment of any spot on Earth for Professor Emma Hallbar. Professor was a new title for her, and one she had taken reluctantly.

Several Universities had offered her a position and she had never even thought of accepting any of them. Recently, however, she had accepted a position at the University in Tahiti, because it was now being reopened. She had done it for their benefit to bring her name to their faculty, which would make their fundraising easier, even if she was only loosely affiliated with the Department of Physics.

She was the now the newest member of the National Academy of Sciences (NAS) of the United States of America. A special presentation of this honor was scheduled for tonight.

She was experiencing an overwhelming wave of emotions about the restoration of the land of her birth to a place of beauty and stability. It represented the pinnacle of her life's work.

She also enjoyed the absence of protestors. She had been at conferences over the past few months and had seen no dissenters recently...at last.

The day held far less value for her self-esteem than the same event would have when she was younger. In the case of her National Academy Membership, it was the journey that mattered, not the destination. She feared the journey was largely over. What could she do next? Where did she go from here?

Thoughts kept rushing through her head concerning what to do with the rest of her life now.

She enjoyed piano and had even learned guitar as well as drums, but was that enough? Perhaps she could form an all scientist rock band?

She consoled herself with the observation that some members were granted NAS membership for things they had done so long ago that those achievements no longer represented the state-of-the-art. She felt fortunate that her work was an exception to that trend. Her journey resulted in a destination that benefitted every person on the planet. Her destination was a safe planet for all.

The struggle she had gone through, all of the hard work, the bullet in her leg, were all part of the challenge. She had met that challenge, in whatever form it had presented itself. She had suppressed many of her natural instincts along the way for the greater good of all mankind.

She did feel some measure of closure as her parents' ashes were now at rest here on the island. She supposed she always thought of it as their island. Perhaps now that it was inhabited again she would make it a family home, someday.

She found it intentionally ironic that the new structure, in the same location as the old, was named *L'Hotel Éternel.* Every single time someone mentioned that name in her vicinity, she felt a tear form in her eye. They didn't always run down her cheek but they were always there, welling up. Tonight she knew she would have to control it, just as she had done so many times in the past.

She admitted to herself that she was of two minds about this hotel. She was still deeply saddened by the tragic end to the first *Hotel Éternel* and the loss of her parents. But she was proud that now the climate had stabilized enough for the island of Tahiti to have almost reached the population level before super storm Cladis hit.

The view of the new hotel from the front paid homage to the appearance of the original hotel. Like the original, it boasted villas on stilts out over the water. The building visible from the front was eleven stories high, matching the original in height and design. It was topped with an infinity pool offering virtually the same view.

They had even offered her the same penthouse living

space her parents had occupied. She bought the penthouse rather than taking the gift, and hoped to use it for the occasional vacation, but did not think they would make it a home.

There was another wing to the new hotel. Further back on the property, out of view from the front of this portion of the hotel complex, was a new twenty-two-story portion that was even more upscale and known as the *Rahi Luxus*. It boasted an even larger infinity edge pool that took up most of the top of the building. The area offered expansive ocean and island views, a swim up bar, and even a water slide that went down all twenty two floors, where it emptied into the ground level pool behind the building.

She had petitioned the government to ensure that the two buildings were hidden from the line of sight of each another to honor those who perished in 2029. They found a masterful way to do so.

As she entered the hotel on her way back from the beach, Emma once again experienced many simultaneous emotions. The entryway did that to her every time. She thought that the exterior did a reasonable job of honoring the original hotel. But all the differences in the interior, from the woodwork to the fabric on the chairs, jumped out at her.

As she walked past the bar, she was nostalgic for her father's reception desk. She could still see his office door behind it when she came through the door. There was still a door there, but the room behind it was not the same.

As soon as she went beyond the reception desk and entered the eleven-story portion of the building, the entire illusion of the original hotel was gone. This was a different building. She still was happy that it existed, even if it wasn't a perfect replacement for what was lost.

Her thoughts returned to the day ahead. The goal of thermal control had been achieved. A large number of people had worked diligently to solve that problem. She was just the most visible member of a very large team.

The ceremony was really to honor all of them. It was beyond her expectations. It was going to be a bit much for her personal taste. It was to be held in the early afternoon, which would allow it to be viewed in primetime by the United States mainland television audience. This was also the first time that the Grand Ballroom of the *Rahi Luxus* would be hosting the visit of a foreign dignitary, The President of the United States.

President Kamanda Tangata was the first non-native born Commander-in-Chief of the United States. There had been a Constitutional amendment making this a possibility over a decade ago, but she was the first. Some believed that Congress specifically had Ms. Tangata in mind when they passed that amendment. She was an excellent Commander-in-Chief. She possessed more tri-partisan support than any of her predecessors had enjoyed in the decades since the United States became a predominantly three-political-party country.

Much to her chagrin, Emma was the most famous

living scientist on Earth, and the daughter of a world famous mother. The entire event was going to be political. The expected ratings it would receive were too lucrative to miss for the networks, and even the President wanted in on the action.

***

"Citizens of Planet Earth, I am here to present to you the major driving force behind the climate you enjoy. This is the person who has saved millions of people who are viewing this event right now from certain death. I ask Doctor Emma Salvatora Hallbar to join me on stage as I present her with Membership in the National Academy of Science of the United States of America," said the President.

"Oh my God," she muttered under her breath. How did they find her middle name? She had never used it, and as the President said the words she almost didn't realize that she was the person who had been named.

She walked up, shook hands, and tried to keep her vision from going crazy as the lights hit her in the face. She walked to the podium to begin her speech.

"Thank you Madam President, thank you to the National Academy, and thank you to everyone within the sound of my voice. I am grateful for the opportunities I have been given. It is a highlight of my career to be here speaking with you about the era we have entered. It is an era that offers us the opportunity to maintain a better climate, a more stable climate, in which all life, including humanity, can flourish on this planet," Emma said expansively.

She felt like she had spent her entire life addressing anyone who would listen. She could not think of many conversations she had had professionally on any other topic. And she would not miss this opportunity.

"The geological history of the Earth includes the greatest Ice Age of them all. We refer to it as 'Snowball Earth.' There have been other times when the climate was warmer and water covered much more of the land mass than today.

"The Earth's orbit varies our distance from the sun over long periods of time. The sun itself is getting brighter; it is known to be a slightly variable star. This is happening at a rate of roughly six percent every billion years or so.

"Human activity is continuing to increase. We are using an ever-changing mix of energy sources. In the long term many of our current sources of the energy we use every day will change. This will happen as a result of changes in technology, as well as from the exhaustion of non-renewable sources.

"All of these things impact our climate. We have proven that we can control the average global temperature. We have chosen the temperature that was present in the year 2020 as the fixed point we will maintain for the foreseeable future. No matter what the cause of global warming, we can control the amount of thermal energy in the system.

"We must never attempt to control specific weather at specific times in specific places. The weather we experience locally, when examined from a global perspective, is the result of random variations that are essential to heat transportation around the globe, to attempt to alter it as some have suggested, to give out a custom local climate if you will, would throw the entire world into imbalance.

"Our great achievement is that we control the amount of total energy flowing into the earth from the sun. We must commit to that task for the remainder of our time on this planet. We must adapt the amount of control we exercise to changes in the environment and exercise caution in how far we are willing to go.

"The commitment we have made must be a permanent one. If we let down our efforts at any point in the future, it will be more threatening to our climate now that we control it than it was before the system was in place. If we lose our equilibrium we may not survive.

"Every calendar year further from 2020 implies a larger effort to maintain that control we all enjoy. I will dedicate the rest of my life to this maintenance.

"I want to thank everyone who has worked with me to make this happen. I look forward to a future in which humanity can flourish, not just for decades or even millennia, but for billions of years into the future."

The applause was deafening. It continued beyond the time allotted for the network television coverage of the event. The viewers all over the world who had been immersed in the middle of a three hundred sixty degree, three-dimensional event were left with the feeling that they had been right there next to Emma. They were rejoicing in the age of climate stability.

The applause disappeared and was replaced with an advertisement for some kind of energy drink.

***

Logging onto the secure internet link from the penthouse hotel room, Emma could access all data from the Control Center at Mount Imperium. The Control Center itself was not connected to any external network in order to protect against cyber-attack. However data was manually transferred to an internet node outside the mountain facility once an hour. She pored over the most recent climate data. The system was healthy, had triple redundancy, and the capacity to handle the extra greenhouse heating effects anticipated for the next decade. Emma felt calmer than she had since the day her parents were killed by cyclone Cladis. She would permit herself her first true vacation in decades. This would become a delayed version of the planned vacation on Tahiti that had been cancelled when she was in prep school, only this time she was the mom.

Chapter Eighteen

"We shall not cease from exploration, and the end of all our exploring will be to arrive where we started and know the place for the first time."

– T. S. Eliot

Emma had a family to raise. That meant that she needed to work on achieving more of a balance in life, which now included parenting, science, and finally time to pursue a hobby, or even just go see a movie. She wanted to do as well with her children as she felt her parents had done raising her. They needed to understand hard work, and that despite their privileges they had to make their own way.

She had started a new activity: auto racing. She had always loved driving, and now she was enrolled in racing school to learn how to do it well without all of the automatic driving tools that came with the modern cars everyone used in their daily lives. Besides, her kids thought it was fun to watch mommy go really fast.

There were countless analyses of her driving skills, and someone told her there was even a Las Vegas casino taking bets on her crashing into a wall by a certain date. In what some called a publicity stunt she took a flight to Vegas, and with as much media attention as she could bring to the afternoon, bet against the crash.

It took her a while, but she finally had her name on the side of a Formula 1 car. As she squeezed into the seat to take her laps in one of the world's fastest cars, she hoped she would not lose her standing Vegas bet by crashing into a wall. She, of course, would not drive in the race. Full-time drivers half her age had earned that privilege. She was able to take test laps.

She experienced one of the biggest thrills of her life driving that car. She strove for safety, but was still astounded by the acceleration, lateral g-forces in the corners, and the stopping prowess of the braking system. The aerodynamics were not only incredibly efficient, there was additional active down force from a set of five impellers located within the aerodynamic envelope of the vehicle. Her first lap felt fast, but the time over the radio was more than twenty seconds slower than the professional driver had set in a previous practice session using the same car. She spun on her second lap, luckily not coming close to any walls. It did require that she come in for a new set of tires and a very stern pep talk from the team manager. Determined to neither embarrass herself nor damage the car, she settled for a lap less than five seconds slower than best the car had ever done. The team was actually amazed that she managed that.

Scott's own work had attracted serious attention from the science community in the last year. He now ran the climate simulation center for NOAA. The upper atmospheric chemistry data that was being collected as the sunshades began to reduce the sunlight incident on the Earth was astonishing. He had learned more about the upper atmosphere in the last eighteen months than during his entire career prior to that point. His model predicted reactions within the ozone layer that were later found to be in astonishingly close agreement with the data. His career was blossoming, although he would never be as famous in the public eye as his wife Emma, which was something he claimed to be very happy about.

Scott and his team had constructed a model of the formation and evolution of the ozone layer that was unprecedented in detail and accuracy.

They were able to share the intimacy of dinner together, without fifteen other people in attendance, far more often than ever before. That was a relatively new luxury, as they both increasingly became masters of their own schedules.

Scott was the lead scientist on a team that had automated the modeling and simulation runs. They were so computationally intensive that even with computer resources larger and more complex than a human brain, as well as billions of times faster, his latest model ran continuously overnight to simulate, at unprecedented resolution, a week of the evolution of the upper atmosphere. After validating the model with real world data, he was currently pushing his model predictions further into the future of the ozone layer. The simulations had been running for months. The automation allowed him more time at home with the family. He had set thresholds for a few basic parameters of the ozone layer simulation results that would trigger a text message for him if something surprising were predicted. That way his presence on site was not continuously required.

These text messages from his simulation center

occasionally interrupted their evening, or even early morning. Emma teased him that it was worse than a car alarm that was too sensitive to cats walking on the hood. Most of the alerts did not actually require his immediate attention, but worked wonders for his peace of mind. Tonight the text caused him to get up from dinner with a look of shock on his face. "I have to go in," was all he said.

He called later from the simulation center and apologized for leaving.

"This appears very serious," he said in a tone of voice she had not heard before. "The model is predicting a catastrophic decrease in the ozone layer due to the sunshades reducing the amount of ultraviolet light falling on the upper atmosphere," he said solemnly. "I must stay here tonight and dig into this. I am calling in the Center Staff. We will be checking these results all night and pushing it even further into the future, hopefully increasing the time into the future as far as we can, with a slight decrease in resolution, that way we can see if it is only a transient effect."

"I don't understand," Emma said in a shocked high-pitched voice that was completely uncharacteristic of her. "Reducing the sunlight to the 2020 level should only be beneficial." If she understood what he said, her husband had just said that the highly successful temperature control program she had dedicated her adult life to making a reality had a dangerous unintended consequence. It was a consequence that no scientist in the world had even posed as a possibility.

"The UV component of that light is necessary to create the ozone layer. The layer, in turn, prevents most of the UV from reaching the ground by absorbing it at high altitude. Less UV from the sun means less ozone is generated. The model is telling us that the layer is very sensitive to the amount of UV it receives from the sun. In fact, it is telling us that reducing the sunlight just three percent, as we are now doing, will reduce the ozone layer at equilibrium by more than six percent. Unlike the ozone holes located near the poles that were produced by the aerosols that were banned decades ago, this is a global effect. If we cannot find an error in the model inputs, our validated model is making a catastrophic prediction. The long-term effect could be cumulative and reduce the ozone layer by even more than six percent. This could threaten not only everyone unprotected in sunlight, but our food supply, and maybe the rest of the living ecology of the planet.

"I love you and I will call you when I can," he said.

Emma was shattered, and she was home alone. She did not even have the emotional support of her husband's embrace. Her kids were off with his parents. She had never felt so alone in her life. She collapsed onto the floor in tears, dropping the phone next to her.

She was to blame for this.

Her entire professional life had been dedicated to saving the planet. She had always privately thought of it that way while managing to never verbalize it to anyone else, except Scott. She had allowed herself to be increasingly happy and fulfilled since she married Scott, and now she was emotionally crashing. For the first time in her life, she used alcohol to steady her nerves.

"Perhaps this was just a false alarm," she thought to herself. Scott had said that he had to check the model inputs. It was only a model, there was always a chance the prediction would not be correct. But she had never known him to make an error like this. Every prediction he made was conservative in nature. He was the most careful scientist she had ever known. His model was well validated in both the lab and against every bit of real data he could obtain. She had more faith in her husband than she did in herself.

"Denial," she then said to herself. She had passed through grief and denial in record time. Disappointment would not prevent her from acting -- if she broke it, she would find a way to fix it.

Over the next two weeks, she followed Scott's work with great intensity. The most prominent experts in atmospheric chemistry had responded quickly, both out of respect for Scott, and the importance of knowing the answer. This was a prediction that was so extreme that it had to be carefully examined. The implications could be very serious. Everyone wanted to be completely correct, and they needed those answers in the shortest amount of time possible.

Emma did not wait for certainty. She immediately began working with her science team on the sunshade project to work out a response. They would be prepared if Scott was correct.

The fix was actually so simple in principle that she was angry with both herself and all of the prominent reviewers for not insisting that it be done that way from the beginning. This entire crisis could have been avoided.

The solution was to make the sunshades transparent to the UV needed to create a healthy ozone layer while blocking the longer wavelengths that were responsible for most of the greenhouse heating. Doing that was simple in principle, but not so simple in practice. It required the formulation of a new sunshade mixture in liquid form. The large deployed sunshades depended upon absorbing UV to cure and to make them rigid after they were deployed in space.

Emma called Mr. Fox, who had recently retired from Congress and no longer chaired the Committee on the Environment. She could not have anticipated his reaction. He had been extremely supportive during the original process of funding and creating the program. In fact, he thought of it as the crowning achievement of his long and distinguished career.

It was largely for that reason that he took great personal offense at being told there was a major flaw that must be fixed. "If you go public with this Dr. Hallbar," he said with a formality she had never experienced from him before, "your reputation and credibility will be destroyed, along with mine."

She surprised herself by yelling in frustration, "If we don't make these changes, the temperature effect on the climate that caused all of the super storms will seem mild in comparison. Mass starvation from crop failure will be the most serious long-term effect from ozone layer depletion. A time will come very soon when everyone will need protection that completely covers any exposed skin before venturing outside."

She could see Trevor Fox's entire body shake on the video call with some combination of anger and a nervous system disease that had forced him to retire. "I have seen no evidence of any change in sunburns or crop production falling. The sunshades are reaching 2020 equilibrium temperature on average, exactly as *you* predicted. I think it is time for you to step aside, Doctor Hallbar. I think you are starting to find problems where none exist. I suggest that you find new and unrelated challenges, rather than inventing a new one for the sunshade program. I understand you are becoming an automobile racer. I wish you well in that endeavor. Learn to relax and enjoy yourself with those children of yours," he said as he cut the line.

The next day her badge did not admit her through the entrance to the Science Team Offices. She inquired at the front desk, and rather than having the badge issue straightened out, she was escorted out the front door. "Dr. Hallbar," the security sergeant said, "you no longer have access to this building. Your possessions will be sent to you."

Her face had lightened in color, and she appeared very frail and paler than anyone had seen her before.

She woke up in the Emergency Room with Scott standing over her. "You gave everyone a scare," he said with a concerned expression that also contained a hint of a wry smile. "You have been thoroughly examined, and you are an exceptionally healthy specimen of womanhood."

He winked at her; "you did, however, boost the ratings of the news programs that are all broadcasting video of your tumble to the ground on what appears to be a continuous loop."

Over the next month she exercised her skills in public relations. She appeared on several television programs warning that the sunshades must be replaced with a newer design. The news channels interviewed many other experts, and they largely supported her view. But those same experts did not project the rushed urgency that she was pushing so strongly. Phrases like "the sky is falling" and "crying wolf" began to enter any discussion about her plan.

Her reputation was declining rapidly in the public opinion polls that were updated daily. She took the polls very personally. It was not her ego that was upset; it was the knowledge that her political influence was falling that disturbed her.

When she first began the sunshade campaign, the storm frequency and sea level rise had both been measurable evidence that justified her passion. The combination of her passion as well as her personal tragedy when her parents died, along with the many other climate-related tragedies unfolding for the eyes of the world to see, had been too compelling to ignore.

Simulation results, on the other hand, were too abstract to generate the same level of widespread support. She began to understand for the first time how important the tragic drama of storm related deaths and the economic losses brought about by climate change had been to her success in funding a solution.

Now she was viewed as an alarmist. News commentators and late night comedians alike never missed an opportunity to treat her as someone who had once been great, but who now was emotionally untrustworthy.

The next few months were one of the lowest points of Emma's life. Even her children couldn't find ways to keep her happy. She even went to Tahiti with them for a vacation and that only made her feel worse. She barely left the hotel. She took no notice that neither did the other guests, for the most part. Visitors attributed their increased sun sensitivity to the tropical latitude, and spent less time outdoors than they originally planned

She had lost authority, credibility, and respect. She was medicated for her clinically mild depression. "Mild," she mused to herself, repeating the diagnosis. She could hardly function by her standards.

Her phone snapped her out of drowsiness and into a slightly groggy attention. Answering the phone, her slow brain could not follow what was being said. "Slow down," she asked the three dimensional image of her animated husband who was talking with his hands and speaking too fast for her to comprehend what had made him so excited.

"Turn on the news channel," he said, "any news

channel! It has begun."

There was widespread coverage of an epidemic of sunburn. Some of the newscasters were having difficulty reporting this with a straight face. In a world that had an abundance of shocking news to report about terrorism, crime, and scandal, the lead story they were asked to read was about an abundance of people getting sunburned? That made no sense to them.

Then the video began to come in from some of the tropical beaches of the world. The beaches had passed local noon, when the sun's light was most direct.

A man who had taken a nap in the sun on Maui had third degree burns. They had a picture of him in the emergency room being treated for burns from his face to his navel.

A woman who had done the same in Mexico while wearing a fashionable swimsuit with many thin straps looked like her back had been branded.

Players at a beach volleyball tournament were also shown being bandaged and treated for burns alongside an ambulance in the shade of a tall building.

Thousands of people were stressing the capacity of Emergency Rooms in the daylight portion of the globe. A reporter made a conjecture that this would continue as sunrise occurred in other parts of the world. They even blamed the scientists, including her, who had decided, in their words, to "play with the environment like a child plays with tinker toys."

The news anchor was warning everyone to cover up, use sunscreen and as much clothing as possible. Medical experts were being called in for live interviews, but their expertise only extended to advice on treating burns and covering exposed skin.

Behind the over-the-air content, there was a mad scramble to find a scientist who felt qualified to comment on the cause of the epidemic. No one was calling her, and she had tried to warn them. If she turned out to be correct, many public figures would be embarrassed by that fact.

Eventually the journalists began to understand that Scott and his colleagues around the world were the experts they needed to invite. This was a problem with the ozone layer. Everyone was asking, how did this occur so suddenly?

Scott called her and said he would be late as he was headed to the closest television studio to do an interview. He was nervous but she walked him through it and told him to speak in layperson terms as much as he could.

She made some tea and waited, watching for him to come on. She was proud of him and was hoping that he wouldn't be trapped by a reporter trying to make him look like the problem rather than a solution.

"Actually it is neither sudden, nor a surprise," Scott said a bit nervously into the camera. This was his first interview on national television. He had seen her do it many times but his part of being on TV had always been standing next to her. She tried to get him to go on a few times but he had always refused, until today.

"Our models predicted it, and Dr. Emma Hallbar has been promoting the solution as well as sounding the alarm," she wished he hadn't used the word alarm. He went on to explain that while a nonlinear threshold effect was in play, there had been increasing sunburn and UV flux measurements for some time. The threshold effect meant an increase in sunburns should be expected, but it had been increasing for many months already.

She wondered how many viewers understood him. She knew he was exactly right, and hoped the audience would also know that. Crop damage was just starting to appear, but wasn't bad enough yet for the news to cover it. There was also damage to natural ecology, most noticeably in the rain forests.

"The threshold effect is more a matter of news reporting than ozone physics," he said, much to the chagrin of his interviewer. "Our models show that this will get very much worse. The time is past for anyone to venture outdoors without protection from the sun. Much more importantly, crop failures around the world will be dramatic in the very near future. Some portions of the globe will likely experience famine, along with all of the associated political, economic and military implications that come along with scarce food supplies."

***

Straight answered his cell phone knowing before he looked at the called ID that it would be his father on the other end.

"We knew they would not be able to understand enough about the planet to alter it without creating a disaster. It is time to activate the second phase of our action plan," his father said.

"I understand father," Straight replied.

***

A corporate CEO addressed his assembled executives, "we were successful in obtaining the largest share of the Sunshade Program contracts awarded to any single corporation. That has made all of you wealthier thanks to a meteoric rise in our stock price. Now there are two additional stages remaining to grow with the future needs of the program.

"First, the existing sunshades will need to be ejected from their orbit and replaced with a new formulation that does not disrupt the UV which generates the Earth's ozone layer. This is an opportunity to double our cumulative income from the project, and to sustain the peak cash flow for a few years longer.

"Secondly, we will be lobbying and making political contributions designed to implement the plan to increase greenhouse gases and increase even more the scope of the Sunshade Program. It will assure protection against any future global cooling events for generations of our descendents. It will also multiply our contracting volume to build the new larger scope system."

***

Over the next several months many things started to change. Covering up from the sun while making a fashion statement was a challenge some fashion designers relished, and allowed them to sell more of their product by creating an additional mid-season fashion change. A group of high profile designers also created and funded a charitable organization to alleviate the suffering the UV was causing. They did not realize that it would take more than money to alleviate the impending disastrous shortages. Money could not buy food that did not exist because of the UV crop damage.

The U.N. was beginning to take notice. They invited Emma to present her solution to an international panel of science and technology experts. The ozone crisis would affect everyone everywhere, not just those who were typically in the path of extreme weather. No place on the planet was safe from the new solar threat.

Answering questions from a podium in front of hundreds of international representatives while listening to the English translation in her earbud was awkward. Both the time-consuming translation process and the lack of even basic understanding of the scientific issues by many of the delegates made this her greatest public appearance challenge by far.

After this ordeal she had hoped approval would soon follow. But it did not.

International politics wandered into many areas that had very little to do with solving the problem, including examining, all over again, every penny of the funding and site selection issues. She couldn't understand why they felt there was a need for a new launch facility rather than just working with the one that existed, but some of the delegates insisted there should be redundancy before any project was initiated.

During this process, the UV irradiance at the surface of the Earth continued to climb quickly. It was directly tracking Scott's simulations, which proved to be quantitatively correct beyond expectations.

"It is surprising how accurate the simulation has been," he said himself. He fed predictions to other experts who could simulate the consequences of increased UV. Agronomists, economists, political scientists, and military analysts all clamored for data. He supplied the data as quickly as his team could produce reliable predictions.

The predictions were grim. If the ozone layer continued to fall as predicted, over one billion people were likely to starve to death. This scale would dwarf the number of deaths due to the bubonic plague or any other catastrophe in human history. Some in the news media were saying this could turn into a biblical level of destruction. Some ministers were even claiming it to be the wrath of God. There was something about humans interrupting God's plan that she didn't care to listen to in its entirety.

Emma and Scott knew that it was just human arrogance coming back to haunt the planet.

The unequal distribution of food and wealth were projected to cause warfare and suffering on a scale never before seen in human history.

***

It took crop failures in the farm regions of member nations to force the U.N. to act. Then they acted as rashly as they had in delaying her plan. This time, Doctor Emma Hallbar was given absolute authority.

"It is fortunate," Emma said to Scott, "that I have been through this before and know my limitations. I will be calling Cliff Morris."

The disaster hit even worse than predicted. Scott's modeling effort was accurate in predicting the increase in UV level, but the other models that estimated the implications of that rise were entering unexplored scientific territory.

Crops all but disappeared in the tropics, and were badly damaged in many of the more temperate latitudes. Canada and Russia suffered the smallest losses among major food producers, but they could not feed the world. All food exports from the U.S. were halted under emergency powers granted to the President. There were protests as farmers insisted they could get a better price from the international community but the President's priority was the survival of the citizens in his country, not short-term profits. As the experts in many disciplines corrected their models with new data, they began to escalate the predicted death toll to over two billion within a decade.

The news channels were now 24 hour per day horror shows. Emaciated victims of malnutrition were shown carrying weapons as members of military or pirate groups. They were seizing food as part of a short-term tactic that in the long run would worsen the food shortage for everyone. Many of these violent groups did not plan for next year; they only stole food for this year. They often killed the farmers who would have been the source of next year's nutrition. There was a downward spiral as portions of society began to lose their concern for others, and their survival instincts began to override judgment.

Millions had died, and some of the television coverage reminded Emma of Holocaust pictures from the German genocide prison camps of the Second World War that she had seen in prep school. This disaster knew no political agenda, it was simply nature following the rules of physics, chemistry and biology.

***

"I have asked for this monthly air time to keep the audience informed about the state of the sunshade program. This is so that you will know what is being done to alleviate the ultraviolet increase by allowing nature to repair the ozone layer," said Dr. Hallbar simultaneously on almost every major network around the globe. She looked at herself on the monitor out of camera view. She felt like she was aging quickly. She didn't want that to happen. Not when they were so close, she could do this.

"Our highest priority is to restore the UV level from the sun that is incident upon the upper atmosphere to full strength. While it may sound counter-intuitive since UV on the surface of the earth is the source of a great disaster right now, the ozone layer needs solar UV to repair itself so that it will absorb the UV at high altitude. That is our protective layer that has been damaged and must be restored.

"In order to do that, we have sent commands to every sunshade station-keeping system to immediately begin the journey away from the Lagrange point and into interplanetary space. Some will stay in solar orbit, some will be destroyed by interplanetary debris collisions, and some will eventually fall into the sun itself, but the priority is to move them away from our line of sight to the sun. None of them will fall on the Earth, although even if they did, each is of relatively low mass and could not survive re-entry into our atmosphere.

"In three months none of the sunshades currently deployed will be reducing UV at the Earth's upper atmosphere any longer. The NOAA Center for Upper Atmospheric Science has simulated the recovery, and within 18 months crop yields will return to 88% of pre-ozone depletion levels. However, solar protection garments will not go out of fashion. Protecting your skin from sunlight will be recommended for several years, and in the short term will become even more important as the solar UV reaching the ground peaks before the ozone layer repairs itself.

"We are certainly aware that 18 months is a long time, and 88% of the crop yield is not 100%. Millions will be adversely affected in the next few years. Millions may die. But literally billions of lives will be saved because of this necessary step.

"Our job will be done quickly in making it possible for the ozone layer to regenerate. But our task with the sunshade program will have just begun...again. We will still need to mitigate the greenhouse heating that generated so many warming-related disasters until a few years ago when the sunshade program started to operate with full effect.

"We have designed new sunshades that will allow 96% of the ozone generating UV wavelengths to pass through the shade. Since they only shade three percent of the sunlight, we will have 99.88% of the original solar UV present to generate and maintain the ozone layer. This is very close to 100% and will restore the ozone layer well enough that no adverse effects will remain after sufficient time has passed.

"During the next 18 months, we will deploy a new set of UV-transparent sunshades that will still control the greenhouse warming at the 2020 average temperature level. During deployment, there will be a gradual rise in temperature, but it will stay below the 2028 average temperature and then reduce to the

2020 target.

"It will take nearly a decade for the ozone layer to reach 99.4% of its former density. During that time we will keep you updated on progress. During this crisis phase over the next 18 months, I will visit you through television, as often as is necessary to keep you up to date on our progress."

And so Emma concluded her first "State of the Planet Address" as the media would come to call it. Her fame was restored, for better or worse, and her authority exceeded all reason in her view, but she still blamed herself for the current disaster. She would fix it, but the blood of millions was on her conscience.

As she left the studio, it quickly became clear that she was not the only one who placed the blame on her for the planetary predicament. A single shot rang out, and once again she hit the ground while being videotaped by news crews alike. There was blood, and the last thing she remembered was someone screaming about Mother Nature.

Chapter Nineteen

"Only one who devotes himself to a cause with his whole strength and soul can be a true master."

– Albert Einstein

Emma woke up in a hospital for the fourth time in her life. This time she was alone in an intensive care room. She was aware of a tube in her mouth that extended down her throat. It was a very bizarre feeling and she began to panic. An alarm tone was coming from some equipment nearby, but it was not in her line of sight. When she tried to turn her head there was a pain from the equipment extending down her throat deeper than she thought was possible.

After what seemed to be a very long time, a nurse entered the room and spoke to her. "Ah, you have been awake for two minutes and are already setting off your alarms," she said.

"Don't worry, it's a common panic reaction. I am putting Lorazepam in your I.V. to calm you. Don't attempt to speak with the breathing tube in your mouth. I know it is uncomfortable, but you will relax in a moment. The doctor will come by later to have a look. We must leave the tube where it is until he says we can take it out," the woman said, far too clinically for Emma.

She speculated on her condition while she was lying

there, unable to talk, and artificially relaxed. She had no memory of pain. She thought she had heard a loud sound that could have been a gunshot, and someone scream something about Mother Nature, another protestor she assumed. Then she woke up here in this room. The only self-assessment she could manage was that she had bandages across her body and on one arm.

Her impatient personality was not holding up well, since she was unable to speak or move more than a very small amount. Time seemed to stand still...freedom of speech and movement had been taken from her.

She assumed that Scott was not allowed to see her until the doctor cleared the visit. She hoped that he was handling this well. He worried every time she took a car on the racetrack. He would be worried beyond all rationality about her now.

She must have fallen back asleep because the next thing she knew, there was a doctor looking at her chart and the instruments that displayed her condition.

He noticed that she had woken up and asked, "Are you ready to remove that breathing tube?"

She nodded slightly and tried to say "yes," but only an indistinct sound came out around the tube.

"Ok," he said and carefully extracted the tube. "You will be relieved to have this out, but you will also have an irritated throat for a while," he said casually with a slight smile. She didn't feel like smiling, but she did find his informal, calm, professional manner reassuring.

"Please tell me what happened, and when my husband can visit," she said directly with more passion than she had intended.

Again he just smiled slightly, "You have been very fortunate. A rifle bullet passed through your abdomen just below the diaphragm, then through your right arm, narrowly missing anything essential to life. You will have discomfort for quite a while, and will need physical therapy for your arm, but your husband can visit this afternoon, and you should be able to go home this week."

***

Scott appeared shaken when he entered her room. He wanted to hug her, but the nurse had told him he could not. He gave her a gentle kiss. He nervously stroked her hands and her left arm, "I love you Emma."

"I love you Scott," she croaked.

"Now please tell me what's going on," she said with a smile.

Scott knew she loved him, even though he couldn't understand what she had said. They loved each other deeply and would do literally anything for each other. They both knew that, so it was with a sense of emotional security that they quickly and comfortably switched to professional mode. He told her that she had been shot from a building across the street, and the shooter appeared to be one of the people who opposed everything she had ever done professionally.

In the day that followed the attack, five different terrorist organizations attempted to take credit for it. The FBI quickly determined which one it was, and the leaders in the U.S. were the either arrested or the subject of an intensive search. The President ordered an investigation into the organization's international connections as well. They thought of themselves as Mother Nature's protectors and would do whatever they could to stop mankind from meddling. Even if it meant mankind had to suffer.

***

She had been called the second best known scientist of all time just behind Einstein. That was before the UV scandal.

Now Dr. Hallbar was known as the person who saved the planet twice, although she held herself solely responsible for the need to do it twice. Launching the first set of sunshades that blocked the UV and damaged the ozone layer was a shared responsibility that no one anticipated.

It was an "issue" that caused the death of many millions of people, through a combination of starvation, war, and suicide. She fixed it as fast as she could, but people still died. The new sunshades allowed the world to have the climate it deserved.

She was relieved they had finally gotten it right. The ozone was replenishing itself just as it should. The planet was healing.

The U.N. unanimously supported the last budget request. It was easy for the nations who were not paying for it to approve it, of course. But the major economies of the world, which did bear the expense, were also unanimous. The same basic logic applied, and would for the foreseeable future. It was thousands of times less expensive to maintain the system than to suffer the consequences of climate change.

Sure, she thought, there were some fringe people who ran websites claiming that she had caused the problem before the original sunshades had been launched, just so that she could have a giant toy to play with. Looking back at her career, two gunshot wounds, and all of the hours doing things she disliked, she sometimes wished she could spend five minutes in a room with some of those people. Then she would always decide that it was better to just drink a cup of tea as it was a more productive use of time.

Emma found that the program demanded less of her time now that operations were becoming relatively routine. She did meet weekly with her science team, and was rapidly building up the simulation capabilities to insure that if Nature held any more surprises for the ecosystem, they would be recognized and acted upon early.

Scott maintained that the simulation organization should be independent of the sunshade program, in order to insure objectivity. She strongly endorsed that privately, and was slowly moving in that direction, but the funding came through the sunshade program that was so politically popular. Separating the science from operations was going to take time and diplomacy, and carried the risk of reduced science funding. For the time being they were attached administratively, but she made sure the two groups remained independent in practice.

Scott required a very large amount of simultaneous high quality data on the state of the atmosphere in order to make predictions more than several days into the future. He wanted to project not just the average global temperature, but the climate itself. The climate details that interested Scott included the distribution and behavior of air and ocean currents, and the variation in, as well as the frequency of, the major weather events that could be expected.

Accurate local weather prediction more than a few weeks into the future could only be calculated by the huge analog computer that is the Earth itself.

Nevertheless, Scott, Emma, and the combined science teams from NOAA and the sunshade program began to think that some underlying principles were emerging. The difference between mathematical chaos in a computer model, and in-principle unpredictability in the real weather was yielding to a combined theory and simulation.

Some scientist long ago invented the popular story that the presence, or absence, of a butterfly in the jet stream over, say, Russia, would either cause a hurricane to arrive, or prevent it from arriving, at the coast of Florida a week later. Even simple mathematical systems could be that sensitive, but no simulation of the planetary weather had the resolution to test this anecdotal story. However, Scott and Emma were arriving at a conclusion based on their reams of results.

They had formulated an uncertainty principle. They were now attempting to prove that weather prediction had a theoretical limit. It meant that while it is an important effect of global warming, the weather would not necessarily follow one path at any given average global temperature.

The uncertainty principle Scott and Emma and their colleagues formulated had several implications. The simplest one was that it is not possible, even in theory, to predict the local weather more than approximately ninety-one days in advance. The team was uncertain about the exact number itself, but it seemed to be a close estimate. Because accurate modern weather prediction had been stuck at around nineteen days for more than a decade since the 2040's, ninety-one days did not sound like an impossible result. It was a best case and very general limit, applying not just to the Earth, but also to Jupiter, or even the Sun. Since the earth had neither the simplest nor most extreme environment in the universe, it would likely have a limit less than ninety-one days, but longer than the nineteen so far achieved.

"The answer for the Earth is thirty-seven days," announced Scott proudly one evening. Emma was happy that he had this result in time for the keynote address that he had been invited to give in two weeks at the inaugural annual meeting of the newly-formed *United Nations Council on Climate Control*. It was both appropriate and ironic that the first keynote address to the group responsible for climate control would tell them that there is a very finite limit to the amount of control that would ever be possible.

***

Scott's day onstage at the United Nations Headquarters in New York City had arrived. Emma had told him all about her experiences here, but his should be much easier. He was not going to spend days convincing the member countries to fund a major program in order to fix a global problem. He was just going to present an overview of his work to date, and then reveal a new scientific result from the teams he represented. It made his task easier that he had an audience of scientists rather than politicians.

Behind the podium from which he would address the assembly, a 30-foot screen displayed a real-time image from space of the entire globe. The view was centered on NYC, which seemed appropriate since this meeting was located at the U.N. headquarters in NYC.

"Distinguished delegates, I welcome you to this inaugural meeting of science representatives from around the world. Our purpose is to understand the extent to which climate itself can be controlled. Control of the Earth's average temperature is not only well understood, it is implemented and operational.

"Direct control of the average climate is a much more complex problem, and I am here to report that the combined Science Teams of the Sunshade Program and the NOAA have made progress in climate prediction, approaching a fundamental limit in the ability to do so." Scott paused as the audience began to murmur, and then to gesture excitedly.

The volume in the room was becoming distracting, and he stopped to understand the distraction. He turned and looked at the display screen behind him. East of the Caribbean, a huge spiral was forming. He thought momentarily that this must be a recording from the days before sunshade global temperature control. But the date and time digital display clearly showed that it was happening right now.

In one of the glass-enclosed VIP observation rooms, Emma had been watching her husband, but also became distracted by the display. Her unbelieving eyes sent an image along the optic nerve to her brain. Her brain recoiled in recognition. This was going to be the size of Cyclone Cladis. It had appeared quickly, with no warning, and this hurricane wasn't even named yet.

Emma stood up. "Oh God not again!"

***

Closed circuit coverage of the meeting more general

in scope than that provided to television news organizations was made available to selected audiences. It clearly showed the new superstorm.

In the nation's capital, Straight and his father were shocked at this newest storm and stoicly grimaced as they watched. Straight had a tear meandering down his left cheek.

In Dallas, a CEO, his personal secretary, his COO, and his chief of security watched and smiled. They high-fived each other and the CEO slapped his security chief on his back.

SCIENTIFIC REFERENCES FOR TECHNOLOGIES IN THIS WORK OF FICTION:

1. http://www.ipcc.ch allows access to the most recent reports by the Intergovernmental Panel on Climate Change, which contains contributions from hundreds of scientists worldwide. Both executive Summary and detailed scientific reports are available. A summary of the 2014 status is at http://www.ipcc.ch/pdf/assessment-report/ar5/syr/SYR_AR5_SPMcorr2.pdf.

2. Music video performed by Kelly Sweet can be enjoyed at: https://www.youtube.com/watch?v=dOz7MBFdg8I&feature=list_related&playnext=1&list=AVGxdCwVVULXcH_1pq4FSQA6Dxe0OeAyCA

Lyrics by Serge Colbert, Mark Portman, and Victoria Jane Horn are listed at: http://www.metrolyrics.com/we-are-one-lyrics-kelly-sweet.html

3. "Feasibility of cooling the Earth with a cloud of small spacecraft near the inner Lagrange point (L1)," PNAS □ November 14, 2006 ☒ vol. 103 ☒ no. 46 ☒ 17189
Roger Angel's article in the Proceedings of the National Academy of Science is online at:
http://www.pnas.org/content/103/46/17184.full#sec-7

4. "Self-Deployed Space or Planetary Habitats and Extremely Large Structures," Devon G. Crowe, Edward A. Reitman, Prakash B. Joshi, and Kophu Chiang, Final Report, NASA Institute for Advanced Concepts (NIAC), March 2007, online at:
http://www.niac.usra.edu/files/studies/final_report/1314Crowe.pdf.

5. "Self-Deployed Extremely Large Low Mass Space Structures," Devon G. Crowe, Prakash Joshi, Ed Rietman, and Kophu Chang, Briefing for the 2007 NIAC Fellows Meeting, online at:
http://www.niac.usra.edu/files/library/meetings/fellows/mar07/1314Crowe.pdf

6. "Sling Launch of a Mass Using Super-Conducting Levitation", D. A. Tidman, IEEE Trans. Magnetics, Vol. 32, No. 1, pages 240-247, January, 1996 (Submitted Oct. 30, 1994)

7. "Sling Launch of Materials into Space", D. A. Tidman, R. L. Burton, D. S. Jenkins, and F. D. Witherspoon, in Proceedings of the 12th SSI/Princeton Conference on Space Manufacturing, May 4 -7, 1995, edited by B. Faughnan, pp.59-70.

8. "The Slingatron", a magazine article by John Kross in Ad Astra Magazine, National Space Society, September/October 1996, pages 47 – 51.

9. "Slingatron Mass Launchers", D. A. Tidman, Journal of Propulsion and Power, Vol. 14, No. 4, pp. 537-544, July-August, 1998.

10. "Slingatron Dynamics and Launch to LEO", D. A. Tidman, Proceedings of the 13th SSI/Princeton Conference on Space Manufacturing, May 8-11, 1997, edited by B. Faughnan, Space Studies Institute, Princeton, NJ, pp.139-141.

11. "Slingatron Engineering and Early Experiments", D. A. Tidman and J. R. Greig, Proceedings of the 14th SSI/Princeton Conference on Space Manufacturing, May 6-9, 1999, pages 306-312, edited by B. Faughnan, Space Studies Institute, Princeton, NJ.

12. "A Scientific Study on Sliding Friction Related to Slingatrons", D. A. Tidman, UTRON Inc., Final Report for U. S. Army Contract No. DAAD17-00-P-0710 February 20, 2001. Interagency funds transfer from NASA.

13. "The Spiral Slingatron Mass Launcher," D. A. Tidman, CP552, Space Technology and Applications International Forum-2001, edited by M. S. El-Genk, published by the American Institute of Physics, 2001. 1-56396-980-7/01

14. "Sizing a Slingatron-Based Space Launcher," AIAA Journal of Propulsion and Power, M. L. Bundy, D. A. Tidman, and G. R. Cooper, Vol. 18, No. 2, March -April, 2002, p330-337. (Presented earlier at 10th U.S. Army Gun Dynamics Symposium, April 23-26, Austin, TX).

15. "Numerical Simulations of the Slingatron," G. R. Cooper, D. A. Tidman, and M. L. Bundy, AIAA Journal of Propulsion and Power, Vol.18, No. 2, March-April, 2002, p.338-343. (Presented earlier at 10th U.S. Army Gun Dynamics Symposium, April 23-26, Austin, TX).

16. "Slingatron: A High Velocity Rapid Fire Sling," D. A. Tidman, AIAA Journal of Propulsion and Power, Vol.18, No. 2, March-April 2002, p322 - 329. (Presented earlier at 10th U.S. Army Gun Dynamics Symposium, April 23-26, Austin, TX).

17. "Study of the Phase-Lock Phenomenon for a Circular Slingatron," G. R. Cooper and D. A. Tidman, AIAA Journal of Propulsion and Power, Vol. 18, No. 3, May-June, 2002, p 505-508.

18. "Constant-Frequency Hypervelocity Slings", D. A. Tidman, AIAA J. Propulsion and Power, Vol. 19, No. 4, July-August, 2003, pp 581-587.

19. US Patent No. 5,699,779, December 23, 1997, on a "Method of and Apparatus for Moving a Mass", D. A. Tidman.

20. US Patent No. 5,950,608, September 14, 1999, on a "Method of and Apparatus for Moving a Mass", D. A. Tidman.

21. US Patent No. 6,014,964, January 18, 2000, on a "Method and Apparatus for Moving a Mass in a Spiral Track", D. A. Tidman.

22. U.S. Patent No. 6,712,055, March 30, 2004, on a "Spiral Mass Launcher", D. A. Tidman.

23. U.S. Patent No. 7,032,584 B2, April 25, 2006, on a "Spiral Mass Launcher", D. A. Tidman and M. L. Kregel, assignee Advanced Launch Corporation, McLean VA, US.

24. U.S. Provisional Patent Application No. 60/935,138, filed July 27, 2007, on a "Mechanical Hypervelocity Mass Accelerator", D. A. Tidman.

25. *SLINGATRON - A MECHANICAL HYPERVELOCITY MASS ACCELERATOR*, Derek Tidman, ISBN 978-1-4276-2658-5, 2007

26. http:/www.nsf.gov/statistics/nsf10311/pdf/tab54.pdf

www.ingramcontent.com/pod-product-compliance
Lightning Source LLC
Chambersburg PA
CBHW071131170626
46809CB00002B/570